Jaco Jacobs is the most popular and prolific children's author in Afrikaans. He has published more than 140 books, together selling over a million copies, among them *A Good Day for Climbing Trees* (Oneworld, 2018). Jaco is also a well-known columnist, blogger, freelance journalist and translator. He lives in Bloemfontein, South Africa.

Kobus Geldenhuys is an award-winning translator who received the South African Academy for Arts and Science Prize for Translated Children's and Youth Literature in Afrikaans for his translation of the third book in Cressida Cowell's popular children's series *How to Train Your Dragon*.

Jim Tierney is an acclaimed book designer and illustrator. In 2011 he was awarded a New Visual Artist Award, and in 2016 he won a Regional Design Award for Amy Stewart's *Girl Waits with Gun*. He lives in Brooklyn with his wife, Sara Wood.

JACO JACOBS

Illustrated by Jim Tierney
Translated from Afrikaans by Kobus Geldenhuys

ROCK THE BOAT

A Rock the Boat Book

First published by Rock the Boat, an imprint of Oneworld Publications, 2018

Originally published in Afrikaans as *Oor 'n motorfiets, 'n zombiefliek en lang getalle wat deur elf gedeel kan word* by Lapa Uitgewers, 2013

ISBN 978-1-78607-450-8
eISBN 978-1-78607-451-5

Typeset by Fakenham Prepress Solutions, Fakenham, Norfolk, NR21 8NL
Printed and bound in Great Britain by Clays Ltd, Elcograf S.p.A

Oneworld Publications
10 Bloomsbury Street
London WC1B 3SR

Stay up to date with the latest books,
special offers, and exclusive content from
Rock the Boat with our monthly newsletter

Sign up on our website
www.rocktheboat.london

MIX
Paper from
responsible sources
FSC® C018072

For my dad,
who can do long division in his head

Nicknames, a Punch in the Nose and the Death of a Show Chicken Called Kathleen

Everyone thought it was because of the chicken that I gave Vusi a bloody nose, but that wasn't really true. Sure, Kathleen was one of my best leghorns, but I wasn't the kind of guy who would just punch people. Not even for a hen that had taken third prize at the previous Bloemfontein Agricultural Show.

My name is Martin Antonio Retief. Back then I was thirteen years, eleven months and twelve days old. My mum called me Martin, but everyone at school called me Clucky. Even my sister and Uncle Hendrik called me that.

My dad died when I was eleven years, seven months and six days old. At the time he was forty-three years, seven months and two days old. Next to him on the car seat was a frozen *snoek* because my mum had asked him to stop at Pick n Pay on his way back from work and bring us some fish for dinner. The lorry that cut right in front of him was carrying thirty new computers. The computers had been on their way to a school in a poor suburb. All the computers were destroyed in the crash, and Nelson Mandela Drive was brought to a standstill for more than half an hour. I knew that because that was what the newspaper said. I didn't know whether those poor kids ever got new computers. My dad was buried four days later, on a Tuesday. There were sixty-two people at his funeral (not including the minister and the people from Doves Funerals).

I have always loved counting things. But I was actually telling you about Vusi.

This is what happened that morning before school: at 06:47 precisely, I knocked on our new neighbours' door.

Their dog came running round the corner, barked excitedly and jumped up on me. I gave him a death stare.

A guy who looked about my age opened the door. I glared at him too.

'Your dog killed my chicken,' I said.

For a moment he looked surprised. Then he screwed up his eyes suspiciously. It looked as if he hadn't slept much the night before. There were dark bags under his eyes and his head was shaven. I wondered whether he'd shaved his hair to look mean.

To my surprise, I watched him lift a video camera and shove it into my face.

'How do you know it was my dog?' he asked from behind the camera. 'It could've been anyone's dog.' He sounded like a newsperson on TV.

'Is this your dog?' I asked and pointed to the tan-coloured mutt at my legs.

He aimed at the ground with the video camera. The dog flashed a doggy smile at the camera, as if to show that he was innocent. That could have worked, perhaps, had it not been for the white feathers stuck to the side of his mouth.

The boy next door also noticed the feathers. He lowered the camera.

'Oh, not again, Cheetah,' he said. 'What have you been up to?'

The dog gave a little yelp and lay down with his head on his paws.

'Vusi, who are you talking to?' asked a voice from inside the house.

'It's just the neighbours' son,' he replied over his shoulder.

A woman appeared from one of the rooms. 'Oh, hello,' she said.

I swallowed. 'Er...hello.'

She was the most beautiful woman I had ever seen, in real life or in any movie, TV show or magazine. She had blonde hair that came down to her shoulders, a small mole on her upper lip and green eyes that looked like the water in the pond behind our house when the sun was shining on it.

'Vusi, you shouldn't stay up for too long,' she said and disappeared into the house.

'Yes, Miranda,' he called after her, secretly rolling his eyes at me. 'Listen,' he told me, 'I'm sorry about your chicken.'

'Kathleen.'

'Huh?'

'Her name was Kathleen. And last year she won third prize in the leghorn section at the Bloemfontein Agricultural Show.'

'OK, I'm sorry about Kathleen. I don't know how Cheetah got out. If you want, I'll ask my dad to give you money for another chicken.'

And that was when I punched him?

No, wrong. I was seriously peeved, but he didn't give me a chance to tell him what he and his dad could do with their money.

'You're the guy who lives next door, in the house with the red roof?' he asked and raised his camera again. 'Isn't your surname Retief?'

I nodded.

5

He lowered the camera and smiled at me. It wasn't an ordinary kind of smile. It was the kind of smile that could mean something else. But I wasn't any good at stuff like that – detecting when a smile meant something different to a normal smile.

'I know who your mum is,' he said.

I gaped at him in surprise. 'What?'

'Wait here,' he said and quickly disappeared down the passage.

The dog and I eyed each other. Maybe I should have left. But Vusi returned almost immediately. He held something out to me. A piece of paper that looked like it had been cut from a magazine. I took the paper and looked at it. It did indeed come from a magazine. One of those magazines that make money from splashing gossip about soap stars and Hollywood actors. The headline read: *What happened to the stars from yesteryear?* And the article included a small picture of my mum.

'The magazine offers a five hundred rand reward if you can help them trace one of these missing stars…' Vusi said and grinned.

And *that* was when I punched him?

Good guess.

2

Leghorns, an Uncle with a Broken Heart and Two TV Series You've Never Heard of

Leghorn chickens were named after a village in Italy. Most of them are white, but leghorns are known particularly for the fact that they can lay so many eggs. One hen can lay up to 280 eggs a year. That means she can lay on average about 0.767 eggs a day. Except when it's a leap year.

'Clucky, whatever possessed you?'

No, that wasn't me talking to the chickens.

It was Uncle Hendrik, my mum's brother, who was talking to *me*. I knew that, sooner or later, he would find me by the chicken coop. I always sit there when I have some thinking to do. Chickens are good company when you want to think.

'I didn't know the guy was dying,' I muttered and watched Bertha, the oldest hen, chase a cricket.

Uncle Hendrik sighed. 'Clucky, since when do you hit other people?'

He sounded decidedly out of breath after that 'long' sentence. Uncle Hendrik wasn't a man of many words. My mum said he was a good orator at school and he was even the master of ceremonies at her and my dad's wedding. But then someone broke his heart and since then he had lived in a small flat outside our house and helped out on the smallholding, or plot as we called it. And not spoken much.

'I don't want to talk about it,' I said.

Uncle Hendrik nodded. I knew he would understand.

'Fine,' he said and put his cap back on his head. 'But you have to go and apologize. That's what your mum said.'

Bertha pecked at the cricket just before it could escape among a pile of bricks. Immediately, the other chickens came rushing up. On average, a chicken lives for up to eight or ten years. Bertha was already eleven. I was two years old the year she hatched. She was the only one left of the B chickens. Bigwig, the white rooster, had died the previous year. Every year, my dad used to give his chickens names that started with a different letter of the alphabet. Charlotte and the black rooster, Chopper, were a year younger

8

than Bertha. My dad died during the K year, the year when Kathleen hatched.

That morning while I was at school, Vusi's dad had been to our house. He'd talked to Uncle Hendrik. I think I would have punched Vusi even if I had known that he was sick. To teach him to shut his mouth and leave my mum alone.

The day I hit Vusi, my mum was forty-three years, eight months and twenty-two days old. When she was younger, my mum acted in two TV series and a commercial. If I told you the names of the two TV series you'd probably think I'd made them up but they're the actual names – *Spring in the Bushveld* and *This Winter*. My mum always joked that if someone had made a series with 'autumn' or 'summer' in the title, her career would probably have lasted longer. The commercial was for Sno-D-Lite ice cream. Chances are that you've never heard of it – I mean, neither the TV series nor the ice cream. Both series were on television before my elder sister, Cindy, was born. And Sno-D-Lite was taken off the market ages ago.

The day my dad was buried was the last time that my mum left the house. Mrs Moosa from the cafe said that my mum had become too anxious to face the world. She said she had read about it in a magazine, and that you call it agoraphobia. Cindy said Mrs Moosa should stop poking her nose into other people's affairs.

Lena, the one-eyed hen, watched me with her head tilted.

'What?' I grumbled.

She slowly blinked her only eye and made a *buk buk buk buk buk bwaaak* sound.

I sighed. 'Yes, sure, I know. The sooner I get it over and done with, the better.'

3

Weird Groaning Sounds, Old Thrillers and Diseases Named after People

Vusi's father looked surprised when he opened the door. Actually, surprised isn't the right word – he looked more disappointed. Maybe he'd been hoping the child who'd given his son a bloody nose was at least slightly bigger.

I swallowed. 'Afternoon, sir.'

'Yes?' He wasn't exactly oozing friendliness, but I supposed that was to be expected.

'Er...could I maybe speak to Vusi, sir?'

A woman joined Vusi's dad in the doorway. I assumed it was his mum. She didn't look very friendly either.

'What are you doing here?'

'I'm looking for Vusi, ma'am.'

'Haven't you caused enough trouble for one day?' asked the woman. 'I can't believe you have the audacity to come here again! Typical of you children from the plots. Vusi is seriously ill, and you–'

'Hang on, Thandi,' the man interjected.

I was surprised that the woman's name was Thandi. Thandi is a friendly name.

Vusi's dad beckoned me inside. 'Vusi's room is the one at the end of the passage, next to the study.'

Hesitantly, I ventured down the hall. It felt as if the man and woman's eyes were burning holes in my back. I peeped round an open door – seeing a bookshelf and a desk, I assumed it was the study. The next door had to be Vusi's room.

Suddenly I heard a groaning sound from the room that I presumed was his. A horrible, drawn-out groan. I swung around and shot Vusi's dad and mum a worried look, but the sound didn't seem to bother them. A sick feeling crept into my throat. Maybe Vusi's parents were used to the groaning. What on earth was the matter with him?

My heart was hammering wildly as I opened the door. I was almost too scared to look… Vusi was lying on a white bed, his eyes glued to a large TV screen. Again I heard that eerie groan. But Vusi wasn't making it – it came from the TV. Vusi could probably hear my sigh of relief, because he looked in my direction.

'Have a seat,' he said, as if he'd been expecting me. He pointed at the TV screen. 'This is the best part.'

I didn't really have a choice. I sat down next to him on the spotlessly white sheet and desperately hoped that there was no chicken poop on my clothes or shoes.

A black and white movie was playing on the TV. It looked very old. There were grey lines across the screen and the actors sounded as if they were speaking through their noses and reading their words off a script.

Vusi pressed pause on the remote control. 'Those guys are zombies,' he explained. 'And that one is their master. It's Bela Lugosi, one of the most famous horror actors ever. He controls all the zombies. They work for him in his sugar mill. The guy who's talking to him is a rich man who lives on the island. He invited a young guy and his fiancée to come and visit him. But he's going to ask the zombie master to change the girl into a zombie.'

I looked at him in surprise. 'And then?'

'Then her fiancé will think that she's dead,' said Vusi. 'And once he's left, the sly rich guy can marry her.'

That sounded very complicated to me.

'What movie is this?'

15

'*White Zombie*,' answered Vusi. 'Don't tell me you've never heard about it. It's a classic. 1932. The first ever zombie movie.'

I didn't know what to say, so I said the first thing that popped into my mind. '1932 was a leap year because you can divide it by four.'

Vusi pressed another button on the remote.

Two men started talking while a guy with disgusting goggle-eyes watched them.

Only then did I see the posters on Vusi's bedroom wall. *Dracula. Scream. A Nightmare on Elm Street 4. Friday the 13th. Child's Play.* Along one wall there was a shelf with rows and rows of DVDs. It didn't look like the room of someone who was very ill. It looked like the room belonged to someone who loved weird movies. The only thing that gave away the fact that Vusi was ill was the drip stand next to his bed. I tried not to look at the needle inserted into his arm.

He paused the movie once more. 'I'm Vusi.'

'I know. I'm Clucky. That isn't my real name,' I quickly added. 'But it's what everyone calls me. Except the teachers at school, of course.'

Vusi sat up. 'Listen, I'm sorry about your chicken. And I'm sorry for what I said about your mum. I won't really let the magazine know where she lives.'

I nodded. 'I'm sorry about your nose. It was the first time I hit someone, honest.'

He grinned and rubbed his nose. 'Really? You punched me like a pro.'

I didn't have an answer to that. Again, my eyes wandered to the needle in Vusi's arm.

'Feel free to ask,' he said.

'What?' I asked guiltily, pretending not to understand what he meant.

'Feel free to ask if it hurts.'

My cheeks felt hot. 'Does it?'

He shook his head. 'No, it only hurts when she sticks the needle in. I mean, Miranda. She's my nurse.' He gave me a challenging look. 'So ask whatever you want to know.'

'What?' I asked.

'Like what's the matter with me.'

I said nothing. But I felt like an idiot for having thought that his head had been shaved to look mean.

'Lymphatic cancer,' he continued. Strangely enough, he said it the way you would say any ordinary words.

'Is it bad?' I couldn't think of anything else to ask. And I was scared that he would tell me again that I could ask him anything.

He nodded. 'It's a kind of blood cancer. There are many types of lymphatic cancer. The type I have is called Hodgkin's disease. I think it's quite dumb.'

'What?' I asked for the third time. I was sounding like one of my mum's old-fashioned records that had got stuck.

'To call a disease after yourself. Why did the Hodgkin guy do such a stupid thing? And it's the same with Alzheimer's and Parkinson's – all those diseases were named after people.'

'I've never thought about it like that. If you discover a disease and name it after yourself, everyone who gets it will hate your name.'

'Exactly.'

We watched the movie for a while.

The zombie master was giving the rich man something to put into the girl's wine. Then he stared into space. 'Send me word,' he said with an affected voice, 'when you've used it.' And then the weird groaning started once more.

Vusi pressed pause again.

'I'm going to make a movie,' he said. 'You can be in it if you want.'

4

Green Beans, Happy Numbers
and a Bedroom Door

'Thank you, Lord, for this food, and bless the hands that prepared it. Amen.'

It always felt strange to hear my mum pray. She said grace in her actress voice. With your eyes closed, you could almost imagine what she had looked like way back, in that black swimsuit in *Spring in the Bushveld*. I was so glad no one really remembered that TV series any more. The thought of other people seeing my mum in her cozzie made me uncomfortable.

The other strange thing about grace at meals was that Mum was blessing her own hands – after all, she had been the one who 'prepared it'. Once I prayed, 'Dear Lord, bless us all, and bless this meal, worms and all', and my mum forbade me from ever saying grace again. Uncle Hendrik bluntly refused to. And Cindy was hardly ever home at mealtimes any more.

We started eating in silence. I suspected Mum wanted to punish me for what I had done to Vusi that morning because she dished up a mountain of green beans for me. She knew I hated green beans. And there were peas as well. I actually liked peas, but I always had to count them before I could eat them. On Mum's plate there was only a small helping of everything – green beans, peas, chicken stew, potato salad. She saw that I was staring at the food on her plate and put down her knife and fork.

'You spent a long time at the neighbours' this afternoon,' she said.

I nodded and shoved a fork heaped with green beans into my mouth. It tasted like something that had floated in dishwater after all the pots had been washed. Not that I had ever eaten anything that had floated in dishwater. That was just a guess.

'I hope you apologized properly.'

I nodded again. I knew my mum was dying of curiosity to hear what had happened at Vusi's place. But if she wasn't going to ask, I wasn't going to tell.

That served her right for the heap of green beans.

'What disease is the boy suffering from?' Mum changed her tactics.

I answered without looking at her because I was busy counting the peas with my fork. 'Hodgkin's disease. It's a type of cancer.'

That shut her up for a while. There were thirty-one peas on my plate. Thirty-one is a prime number because it can only be divided by one and by thirty-one. It's also a happy number. At the beginning of the year, when I told the new maths teacher, Mr Faure, that 368 was a happy number, he snorted and asked whether I was superstitious.

Happy numbers have nothing to do with super-stition. Dad taught me to think of happy numbers when I was struggling to fall asleep. When you square the digits in a happy number and add them up, and then do the same with every new number you get, the final answer will always be one.

Thirty-one is easy to work out:

$3^2 + 1^2 = 10$

$1^2 + 0^2 = 1$

'I'm going to visit Vusi again, tomorrow afternoon after school,' I said after forcing myself to swallow the last few green beans.

My mum looked sceptical. 'So, are you friends now?'

'I don't know.'

She seemed to think about this for a moment. 'As long as you don't make a nuisance of yourself,' she warned. 'If he's that sick...'

'His nurse said it was OK,' I said while carrying the plates to the sink. 'We're going to make a movie.'

I went to bed early but found it hard to fall asleep – maybe because so many things had happened that day. It was the first time I had given someone a bloody nose. I had buried Kathleen. And the next day I was going to start making a movie with the neighbours' son.

I noticed a car's headlights through the curtains, and then heard Cindy sneaking into the house – even though Mum always told Bruce not to bring her home later than ten. The red digits on my alarm clock flashed 23:41.

Was 2,341 a happy number?

$2^2 + 3^2 + 4^2 + 1^2 = 30$

$3^2 + 0^2 = 9$

$9^2 = 81$

$8^2 + 1^2 = 65$

$6^2 + 5^2 = 61$

$6^2 + 1^2 = 37$

$3^2 + 7^2 = 58$

$5^2 + 8^2 = 89$

$8^2 + 9^2 = 145$

$1^2 + 4^2 + 5^2 = 42$

$4^2 + 2^2 = 20$

$2^2 + 0^2 = 4$

$4^2 = 16$

$$1^2 + 6^2 = 37$$

Thirty-seven again. The moment an answer is repeated, it means that you haven't found a happy number.

The alarm clock changed to 23:42. I sighed and got up to get a glass of water.

I wasn't the only one who was still awake at that time of the night. In the lounge the bluish light of the TV was glowing. Mum was lying stretched out on the couch. She was watching one of those long life-insurance commercials, the kind that flashed a phone number on the screen every couple of minutes. 'Nobody likes talking about death,' said the man on the TV. 'But what will happen to your loved ones one day when you are no longer there? Will they be able to enjoy the same quality of life, or...'

I silently turned around and slunk back down the passage. I stopped at my parents' bedroom. The door was closed. Since Dad's death Mum hadn't slept in their room. All his clothes were still in the wardrobe. Suddenly, I missed him so badly that my throat felt as if it was lined with sandpaper.

I drank my glass of water in the bathroom and got back into bed. When I finally fell asleep, I dreamed of zombie chickens.

5

Seven Plot Plodders and a Spluttering School Bus

Not all plots look shabby and run-down, or have wrecks of old cars scattered all over the place, half-dead trees and rickety chicken coops guarded by vicious mongrels.

Some plots boast smart houses with high fences around them and lawns that look like they've been clipped with a nail clipper. And rose bushes. But those weren't really the kind of plots you found in Estoire.

The kids at school called us the plot plodders. And the fact that we were driven to school and back in a bus that was an old rust bucket didn't exactly help. There were seven of us who took the bus every morning and every afternoon:

1. Me.
2. Patrick, who wore the thickest glasses I'd ever seen and always reeked of onions because

his mum ran a pickle factory from their backyard shed.

3. Safraaz, whose dad owned the garage and cafe, and therefore thought he was better than the rest of us.

4. Waylon, who played prop for the school's first rugby team, even though he was only in Grade Ten, and whose mum packed him an entire Shoprite bag full of snacks every day. Waylon used to boast that he ate four eggs for breakfast every morning. Actually, I shouldn't complain, as his mum was one of my best clients – she bought three dozen eggs every week. But Waylon also liked bragging about the after-effect of all those eggs. We always travelled with the bus windows open, no matter how cold it was.

5. and 6. The blonde twins, Mandi and Jolandi, who were in Grade Nine and always shared an MP3 player, with the one earphone in Mandi's ear and the other one in Jolandi's. Sometimes I thought they shared a brain as well, but I never told anyone about that.

7. And Chris, the only one among us who was never called a plot plodder openly because she once gave the captain of the first rugby team a shiner after he dared to call her that.

Yes, Chris was a girl. She was slightly built and she had large, dark eyes and long blonde hair that all the boys were desperate to touch (but you would've been really dumb to dare to try that). And everyone knew that her eldest brother was in jail.

The small bus coughed and spluttered in the cold.

'Ferreira, get a move on!' Mr Oldman called and hooted like crazy as Patrick came running towards the bus with his bag over his shoulder. 'One day you'll be late for your own funeral!' He said that every morning.

'Sorry, sir,' mumbled Patrick. He mumbled that every morning too.

Patrick was lucky. He was the last one the bus picked up. It meant that he got the worst seat (up front, next to Mr Oldman), but by the time we stopped at their plot the bus had warmed up and didn't stall so easily. That morning my hands were burning from the cold – we'd had to get out twice to push.

We shared the small bus with the retirement home. During the day it was used to take old people to the shops. That was why *Silver Years Home* was painted on the side of the bus. Once, Mandi and Jolandi had tried to bribe Waylon to paint over the words.

Mr Oldman's nickname was Ollie the One-Armed Bandit but none of us dared call him that. When he lost his temper you had to watch out. He once dropped Waylon in the middle of nowhere and drove off because Waylon had dared joke about Mr Oldman's arm. People said he had lost his arm in a car accident when he was still young. Apparently he had been a provincial tennis player before the accident. Watching him drive was quite something. When he changed gears he gripped the steering wheel with one bony knee.

The bus pulled away with a growl. Everyone was quiet that morning. A Sotho newsreader's voice was droning on through the crackling loudspeakers. The bus radio was ancient and you could no longer change the stations but Mr Oldman still switched it on every morning. Patrick was the only one who understood some Sotho because, when he was small, his family had a Sotho housekeeper who taught him some of her language. Sometimes he would tell us if there was important news. The broken radio was one of the reasons why the twins were always listening to their MP3 player.

I stared out of the window at the bare trees and dry brown grass. On the side of the road the frost was still shiny white. Patrick had a cold and was sniffing every now and then.

What if a real zombie plague broke out and the seven of us – eight, including Mr Oldman – were the only survivors? I tried to imagine what it would look like if the groups of people waiting by the roadside for buses and taxis were all bloodthirsty zombies.

Usually Mr Oldman would lose his temper in traffic and then he'd swear under his breath and use his only hand to give people the finger. So I figured he would run over and kill some of the zombies if he was angry enough.

I wasn't so sure how well the rest of us would cope.

Waylon was big and strong enough. If he got hold of the tyre lever or something he could smash a few zombie heads in.

Patrick would be useless against a mob of zombies. But maybe he could keep the zombies at bay with that onion stench. No, wait – it's actually vampires who are supposed to be the ones who hate garlic.

Safraaz would probably just stay in the bus and expect the rest of us to jump out and do the dirty work, killing all the zombies.

The twins wouldn't be of much use either; they would just yell and flap their hands in the air, the way a lot of girls do in horror movies.

Chris...

'What're you looking at?' she asked.

My face felt hot. 'Nothing,' I muttered and quickly looked away.

To hide my embarrassment I started counting the cars driving by. When I reached thirty-seven, I threw her a furtive glance. She was sitting with a slight smile on her face, staring out of the window.

6

Vusi's Movie

'*The End of the World.*' Vusi nodded.

'What kind of name is that for a movie?'

'It says exactly what it's about,' said Vusi. He picked up a sheet of paper from his desk. 'Take a look...'

'What's that?'

He sighed and rolled his eyes. 'Can't you see? It's our poster, man! And that isn't all...' He took a bottle from the drawer in his desk.

'Erm...' I said and looked at the red stuff in the bottle. I stopped myself from asking what it was.

'Fake blood,' announced Vusi proudly. 'The kind they use in movies. I got the recipe on the internet. You use red food colouring, flour, gelatine–'

'Vusi, would you like some fruit juice?' Miranda poked her head around the door. 'Hi, Clucky,' she added. Her hair was tied up in a ponytail. I still didn't know how she'd found out my name. Maybe Vusi had told her.

'That would be nice, thanks,' said Vusi.

I just nodded. My throat suddenly felt dry.

'How are you feeling?' Miranda asked Vusi, sounding concerned.

'I'm OK,' he said impatiently. 'I'm trying to explain to Clucky how to make fake blood.'

'Don't you have to go to school at all?' I asked after Miranda had left.

'They've been homeschooling me,' Vusi explained. 'Since the beginning of this year.'

'Wow, you're lucky.'

Vusi looked at me without saying a word and shook his head.

I felt like an idiot. 'Sorry...I...I mean, I wouldn't mind being homeschooled.'

He laughed. 'My mum is worse than any teacher I've ever had. Come on then, do you want to see what I'm going to do with the blood or not?'

I nodded.

'Hold out your hand. Wait, first take off your jacket.'

I quickly took off my jacket and held out my hand. He opened the bottle of fake blood, picked up a brush from his desk and started to paint the blood on my hand. It was cold and felt like jelly. When he was done, he took a step back to look at his handiwork. I wiggled my fingers. The fake blood felt sticky.

Miranda almost dropped the fruit juice when she returned. 'Good grief! That looks terrible! Clucky, we have to get you to casualty immediately – you've already lost too much blood.'

'It's fake blood!' I quickly pacified her.

She burst out laughing. 'I know, but it looks very real. And very creepy! As if your hand's been in a mincer.'

Fortunately, I'd never seen anyone whose hand had been in a mincer. But Miranda was a nurse, so maybe she had.

'She's nice,' I said when I was sure that Miranda was out of earshot.

Vusi nodded. 'And very expensive.'

'What?'

'D'you know how much a home nurse costs? My parents could never afford it. My grandpa's paying her.'

'You have a rich grandfather?'

'Yep. My mum's dad. But it's been years since I last saw him. He and my mum no longer speak to each other. When he heard that I was sick, he offered to pay for a nurse. At first my mum didn't want to accept the offer, but my dad convinced her.'

I wasn't quite sure how to respond to that, so I kept quiet.

'So, are you ready?' asked Vusi.

I frowned. 'For what?'

'For the first scene of the movie.' Vusi looked around his room as if he was seeing it for the very first time. He seemed to be concentrating hard. Then he picked up the video camera from his bedside table.

'Can I go and wash my hand?' I asked.

He shook his head. 'No, your hand's going to be one of the main characters in this scene.'

It seemed that Vusi had planned everything right down to the last detail – the way you first work out a difficult maths problem in your head before you start writing down the solution. First he drew the curtains so that it was dark in the room. Then he positioned himself in front of the poster of *A Nightmare on Elm Street 4*.

He switched on the camera, raised it to his face and said in a shaky voice, 'One day, your life is normal and boring. And the next – *ZAP!* – a zombie plague breaks out. Zombies every-where in the streets. Your teachers at school. Your best friends. Your neighbours. Your mum and dad. Everyone...zombies!'

I held my breath when he stopped. He seemed to have taken a moment to think about what to say next. He was staring at the camera.

I heard something tiptoe behind me on the

wooden floor. I swung around and exhaled softly. It was only Cheetah.

It looked like the dog was exactly the inspiration Vusi had been waiting for.

'The only thing you have left in this world is your dog.'

He turned around and pointed the camera at Cheetah. The dog barked excitedly and tried to lick the camera.

'Your faithful old dog,' said Vusi in his camera voice. 'Your faithful dog, Killer, who will defend you to the bitter end. Man's best friend.'

Cheetah made a strange yelping sound. Maybe he was wondering why his name had changed to Killer. Or maybe he was wondering whether he really would defend his master 'to the bitter end' after everyone on earth had changed into zombies.

'Hey, Killer, watch out!' Vusi screamed unexpectedly.

Cheetah and I both jumped with fright. Cheetah barked viciously.

'The window!' Vusi shouted and jumped aside.

Puzzled, I looked at the window.

'OK, now it's your turn,' Vusi said in his normal voice. He had switched the camera off.

'Huh?' I asked.

'Your hand, dude,' Vusi said impatiently. 'Now your zombie hand has to appear through the window. Go and stand outside the window and wait until I shout "Action!" OK?'

7

Loitering Around, Getting up to No Good, Lotto Numbers and a Leather Jacket

'They broke into Moosa's cafe again over the weekend,' Mum announced on Tuesday evening as we were sitting in front of the TV. Her voice sounded shaky. 'It was the second time this month.'

'Yes, I know,' I said and took a bite of my sausage roll without taking my eyes off the TV screen.

There was canned laughter about a joke I'd missed. As always, only a faint chuckle came from deep inside Uncle Hendrik's chest. It always sounded like his laughter was wrapped in cotton wool.

'I read about it in the police newsletter,' said Mum. The police delivered a monthly report to all the plots to inform everyone of criminal activity in the area. I think my mum was the only person who read that report from top to bottom. After that she would spend an entire week worrying about all the crime.

'Safraaz told me,' I said.

'Oh, yes,' Mum said. 'I forgot Moosa's son also goes to school on the bus.' She sighed. 'They suspect a gang of young people is behind the burglaries. Goodness me, the youth of today... They struggle to find work, they loiter around and get up to no good. There's a complete lack of discipline in our homes and schools. What on earth is happening to this world of ours?'

'When did you last set foot outside this house?' asked Cindy with a grunt. 'You have no clue what's going on in the world.'

I hated it when Cindy spoke to Mum like that, but felt it best to keep quiet. Since she'd started her course in beauty therapy at the beginning of the year, we hardly ever saw her. Most evenings Bruce fetched her, and then they partied in the city until who knows what time at night. Mum's complaints were a waste of breath.

'Maybe I don't know what's going on in the world,' Mum said softly. 'But what I do know is that I would never have dared to speak to your grandmother like that when I was your age.'

'When you were *my* age–' Cindy started in a

shrill voice, but fortunately the doorbell rang at that very moment.

Cindy jumped up to open the door.

'Evening, evening,' announced Bruce. 'Sorry for pitching up during dinner.'

'That's OK, we just finished eating,' Cindy said quickly. She hadn't touched the sausage rolls that Mum had made.

'How's the egg entrepreneur?' he asked and ruffled my hair as if I was five years old. 'Mark my words, Cinds, before your little brother leaves school, he'll have made his first million with those chickens of his.'

'Let's go,' Cindy said curtly and picked up her jacket.

But Bruce spotted the Lotto ticket on the small side table in the lounge. 'Is Uncle playing the Lotto again? Nice! I hope you'll share your fortune with me when your ship comes in.'

Uncle Hendrik didn't say a word. Nor did I.

Bruce put his arms around Cindy's waist. 'Well, off we go, you and I.'

'Cindy got home goodness knows what time the other night, Bruce,' said Mum. 'You know my rule...'

Bruce laughed. 'Sorry, Auntie. Everything's hunky-dory. Don't worry, she's in safe hands. C'mon, Cinds.'

They walked out with their arms around each other and, a moment later, Bruce's pickup truck roared outside.

'That boy is much too big for his boots,' said Mum.

Uncle Hendrik picked up the remote and turned the TV louder. The Lotto programme had started.

'Thanks for the food, Mum,' I said quickly.

I grabbed my plate to go and put it in the sink. I couldn't watch the Lotto draw on TV. The times I did watch while Uncle Hendrik checked his Lotto numbers, I had lain awake for hours afterwards because the sums made my head spin. The chances of guessing all six numbers correctly are 1 out of 13,983,816. You're seven times more likely to be struck by lightning. Once during a computer lesson at school, I read on the internet that if you bought a Lotto ticket every week you'd have to play for about 269,000 years before you could be sure to win the jackpot.

I wondered what Uncle Hendrik would do if he won millions of rands. We certainly weren't rich but Mum always said we had enough to get by. Dad's life insurance had been enough to pay off the plot, and his pension provided for the rest. Uncle Hendrik also earned some money as he was the verger at church. And thanks to my egg money I had enough pocket money. But I saved most of that. Soon my savings would be enough...

On the way back from the kitchen I walked past the lounge and peeped inside. Mum and Uncle Hendrik were still glued to the TV. This was my chance.

I tiptoed down the passage and stopped in front of Mum and Dad's bedroom. I opened the door and quickly slipped inside. The room smelled musty after having been closed for so long. I took the torch I had sneaked out of a kitchen drawer from my jacket pocket and flicked it on. The torchlight played over the neatly made double bed with the green duvet. I felt like a real criminal when I opened the wardrobe door. Mum's words about young people loitering about and getting up to no good echoed in my head.

At the bottom of the wardrobe Dad's shoes were arranged in neat rows as if they were still patiently waiting for him to return and put them on. His shirts and jackets were lined up neatly on the rail. I reached out my hand to touch them and then pulled back. The wardrobe, the whole room, felt like an exhibition at a museum that no one was allowed to touch.

I shone the torchlight over the row of clothes. At the end of the row I saw what I was looking for. The black leather jacket Mum gave Dad the Christmas before he died. 'Next Christmas I want the motorbike that goes with this,' he teased. He was crazy about that jacket.

'We need a jacket,' I whispered softly. 'For Vusi's movie.'

I don't know why, but for a moment I stood still, as if I was expecting to hear an answer.

The house was as quiet as a grave, apart from the voice on the TV in the lounge. 'It's number nine – and everything's fine with lucky number nine!'

The leather felt cool under my fingers when I took the jacket off the rail.

8

A Bike, an Escape and
an Action Scene

'Over my dead body.'

Vusi gave Miranda, who was standing with her hands on her hips, an imploring look. Even Cheetah took notice of the pleading face he pulled. 'Please, Miranda. My mum and dad don't have to know about it.'

'Vusi, you're not even supposed to be out of bed. I'm not going to allow you to get on a bike,' Miranda said in a strict voice.

'It's *my* quad bike,' pleaded Vusi. 'It was my Christmas gift last year. Dad never used to mind when I went riding on my own on dirt roads.'

'That was before you got ill.'

'But I'm feeling fine today.'

It was true: he looked much better. He said he wasn't feeling tired, and there was some colour in his cheeks.

'C'mon, Miranda, it's going to mess up this

whole thing. I *have* to make my getaway on the quad, otherwise the zombies will get me.'

'You'll just have to think of another way to get away from the zombies, Vusi,' Miranda said with a *that's it* voice. 'I don't mind if you boys want to stay outside for an hour or so, but then you have to come inside. And don't take off that jacket – you'll get sick.'

'Can't we just shoot a different scene today?' I asked after Miranda had gone back into the house.

Dad's leather jacket was way too big for Vusi. It looked like he was drowning in it.

'Just one spin on the bike,' he said with a sigh. 'I want to get a shot of Cheetah and me riding in the *veld* and a zombie almost yanking me off the bike.'

I frowned. 'I'm not really getting the story. What exactly is going to happen? In the movie, I mean.'

Vusi smiled. 'Just wait, you'll see. Look what I got…' He rummaged in his backpack and pulled out a rubber mask. 'This is for you. For the scene in which you almost drag me off the bike.'

The hair on the back of my neck stood up when I saw the zombie mask. The eyes were a spooky, milky white and part of the zombie's bloody jaw was hanging to the side.

Cheetah growled threateningly.

Vusi looked at his watch. 'My dad only gets home from work at five and my mum's gone shopping. She'll be away for at least an hour...' He pulled a key out of his pocket and twirled it round his finger.

My mouth fell open. 'Oh no, Vusi,' I said anxiously. 'Your parents are going to find out about this.'

'By the time they find out, we'll have shot the scene,' he said. 'C'mon, the quad is in the garage.' He picked up his backpack and started walking in that direction, with Cheetah at his heels.

I hesitated for a moment before I ran after them.

Cheetah's tail started wagging when he saw the quad bike and he barked excitedly.

'Shut up!' Vusi scolded.

'Vusi, I really don't think this is a good idea...'

What if something happened to him? He could fall off the quad. Or have an accident. Or get sick. What was I supposed to do then? What would I tell his mum and dad?

'Relax,' he said. 'Quick, open the garage door. Once we're outside, you can jump on.'

The door creaked open, making a terrible noise. Then the quad bike roared to life. Vusi revved the engine loudly once or twice and rode out of the door, with Cheetah on the back.

'Jump on!'

I made it just in time before he pulled away, scattering gravel, and I had to cling on for dear life.

'Vusi!' called Miranda. 'Vusi, come back! I told you not to–'

The quad's engine swallowed the rest of her sentence.

'Whooo-hoooooo!' screamed Vusi.

Cheetah barked elatedly. He was obviously used to riding on the quad with Vusi.

We raced around the back of the house and followed a bumpy little dirt road that snaked through the dry winter grass. The cold wind was whooshing in my ears. The plot that belonged to Vusi's family was much bigger than ours – it had a dam with a few cattle grazing close by and a clump of bare trees that looked as if they were feeling the cold in the pale afternoon sun.

Vusi slowed down and stopped. We were at the boundary fence of their plot.

'Right,' he said and took his backpack off. 'Now we're going to start shooting.'

'Miranda's going to kill you,' I said.

'We can worry about that later.' He scouted the area. 'OK, you're going to put on the zombie

mask and then you have to jump out from behind that tree and try to grab me as I drive past.' He held the mask out to me. 'Go on then, put it on so that I can see if you can walk like a zombie.'

I pulled the mask over my face. It smelled of rubber and I could hardly see through the two little holes for my eyes.

'OK, now walk,' ordered Vusi.

I walked a few steps.

'No, wait, you have to walk like a zombie!'

I took the mask off. 'How am I supposed to know how a zombie walks?'

He sighed. 'Haven't you ever watched a zombie movie? Look, hold your arms stretched out in front of you,' he explained, 'and then walk with your legs slightly stiff. And say "Ahhh".'

'Ahhh,' I said.

'No, man, not like when the doctor tells you to stick out your tongue. Like, "Ahhhhh!",' he groaned. 'It must sound like you've been dead for days. And you're hungry for human flesh.'

I'd never been dead or felt like eating human flesh, but I pretended to understand exactly what he wanted.

'AHHHHH!' I growled.

'Much better.' Vusi sounded satisfied. He took the camera from his backpack. 'OK, let's start. First listen to what I'm saying into the camera, then you'll know exactly what you need to do. I'll tell you when to put on the mask and go and hide behind the tree.'

He cleared his throat and stood next to the quad bike. Then he held the camera in front of his face. 'Three…two…one…action!' he said and pressed the red button on the side of the camera. 'Fortunately, Killer and I could escape in time.' He swung his camera around to Cheetah, whose tongue was hanging out from all the excitement. 'But it was touch and go. If one of those zombies gets hold of you, it's curtains. Just one bite and you'll also change into one of them. Had it not been for the quad…' he aimed his camera at the bike, '…we would have been done for. Oh well, we have to hit the road again. We need to find a place to hide before it gets dark. If we're outside after sunset, both of us will be goners, Killer.' He rubbed his dog's ears. 'And…cut!' he called and switched off the camera. 'What do you think?'

'Erm… I think you're very good,' I stuttered. 'I mean…to just talk off the top of your head like that.'

'I thought up the entire scene last night while lying in bed. C'mon, we have to hurry – my mum will be home soon and then there'll be trouble.'

He didn't really sound worried though. I sort of understood why – it wasn't as if his mum could ground him or anything like that because he had to stay home all the time anyway.

We walked a short distance to one of the trees and Vusi showed me where to wait. With the tip of his shoe he drew a line in the dust and told me to put on the mask.

'Remember, don't jump out before I've crossed this line.'

I nodded. My face was glowing hot under the zombie mask. From behind the tree I watched Vusi walk back to the bike. He and Cheetah got on and the engine started roaring.

'And...action!' shouted Vusi.

The quad bike was approaching fast. I tried to remember how I was supposed to walk and what I had to do. When Vusi crossed the line, I stumbled forward from behind the tree.

'AHHHHH!' I groaned and grabbed at Vusi.

The next moment I heard an angry growl and something got hold of my trouser leg. 'Let go of me!' I hollered. 'Help! Vusi!' I yanked the mask off my face. 'Cheetah, it's me! Let go!'

Cheetah let go and backed off. Vusi stopped in a cloud of dust and ran back to us.

'Are you OK?'

I nodded. Fortunately I was wearing jeans.

'Relax, Cheetah, it's just a game. Sorry,' he said to me.

'No worries.'

Both of us were quiet when we suddenly heard a noise. It sounded like someone was howling with laughter.

'Hey, who's there?' called Vusi, sounding peeved.

Cheetah ran in the direction of the noise.

There was a movement on the other side of the fence, and someone appeared from the bushes. A girl. Cheetah licked her hand through the wire fence.

She laughed. 'That was officially the funniest thing I've seen in my entire life.'

'Hi, Chris,' I said sheepishly.

9

A Conversation

'A movie? About zombies?' She guffawed again.

'You promised not to laugh if we told you,' said Vusi.

Chris tossed her long blonde hair over her shoulder and smiled at him. 'Sorry. I promise I won't laugh again.'

Vusi looked at me and then at Chris. 'How do the two of you know each other?'

'From the bus,' said Chris. 'We ride to school together every morning.'

'And what are you doing here?' Vusi still sounded slightly peeved.

She rolled her eyes. 'I live here.'

'In the bushes?' I asked, surprised.

'No, Einstein, in a house. This is our plot. Hello-o-o, the one where the school bus stops every morning!'

My face felt as if it was on fire. I didn't understand why I always had to say the first dumb thing that sprang to mind.

'So what's the story?' Chris asked. She looked at Vusi. 'I guess you're the fearless hero of the movie since your head doesn't have a single hair standing on end.'

Vusi said nothing, but he touched his hairless head self-consciously. I immediately felt sorry for him about what Chris had said. And I felt sorry for Chris too because she didn't know he was sick, otherwise she would never have made a joke like that. Hopefully not anyway.

'Vusi is also the director of the movie,' I said to break the silence.

'And the cameraman as well, I see,' said Chris. 'Clucky, it looks like your only part in the movie is to be eaten alive by a dog.'

I wasn't quite sure, but it felt as if she was poking fun at us again.

She leaned against the fence. 'Now tell me, what's going to happen next, now that the dog has ripped one zombie to pieces?'

Cheetah grinned with an open mouth, all innocence – as if he hadn't tried to wolf me down a few minutes ago.

'Vusi is looking for a place to hide for the night,' I said. 'Otherwise the zombies will get him.'

'In the movie my name is Brad,' Vusi corrected me.

Humph. That was the first I'd heard about 'Brad'. I immediately stopped feeling sorry for Vusi. Why hadn't he told me earlier that his movie name was Brad? I thought we were both supposed to be in the movie.

'I'm going to hide in an old shed for the night,' Vusi continued, 'and then I'm going to discover a girl who's also hiding from the zombies.'

I glowered at him. That was also the first mention of *that*. No doubt he was making all this stuff up on the spot.

'And where d'you reckon we'll find an old shed?' I asked. 'And a girl to play that part?'

For a moment Chris stared at Vusi and me with a slight smile plucking at one corner of her mouth and a sparkle in her eye. Seeing her like that, it was difficult to imagine that she had given a rugby player a black eye.

'I know the perfect place,' she said. 'A dilapidated old shed...'

'And you're a girl,' Vusi added.

'Huh?' asked Chris, and then she started to laugh. 'Oh no! Don't even think about it!'

10

The Word 'Dead' and the Number Zero

To me, words are more difficult to figure out than numbers. Take, for example, the word 'dead'. We say something is 'dead easy' but why? Who says dying is easy?

'Dead quiet' makes more sense to me. But on the other hand, maybe death isn't quiet at all. Maybe you hear music all the time when you're dead. Or maybe you hear what other dead people are thinking. Or maybe you hear what the people who are still alive are thinking. Anything is possible. It isn't as if the first guy who thought of calling something 'dead quiet' knew what you could hear when you were dead.

I lay on my bed with my eyes wide open, not moving. It's strange, the moment you think it's so quiet that you can't hear a thing, you start hearing all kinds of things. The fridge humming in the kitchen. The wind stirring outside. A dog barking somewhere in the distance. One of the chickens in the coop, making a sound in its sleep.

I wondered if Vusi also thought of death sometimes.

The doctor said that there was a 40% chance he would get well again. The doctor hadn't told Vusi that himself, but he overheard his mum telling someone else on the phone. It meant that there was a 60% chance that he would die. I wondered how doctors work out something like that. It didn't sound to me like their calculations were very accurate. Why did no one ever have a 39.426% chance to get well again?

Miranda was very angry when we got home on the quad bike. So angry that she threatened to tell Vusi's mum what we'd got up to.

'What if something had happened to you? How would I explain that to your mum?' She sounded ready to burst into tears.

'But nothing happened to me,' Vusi said. 'Why can't you people understand? I don't want to spend my days in that stupid bed. I'm not dead yet!' Vusi chucked his backpack to one side and ran into the house.

Miranda and I remained outside, alone.

'I won't tell Vusi's mum,' she told me. 'But please don't let him do something like this again.'

Walking home, I felt guilty, as if it had all been my idea.

Lying in bed that night, I realized I had to get some sleep, otherwise I'd be deadbeat the next day. The word 'dead' again. But I guessed people who died were deadbeat.

The electronic digits on the alarm clock said it was 01:33.

$$1^2 + 3^2 + 3^2 = 19$$
$$1^2 + 9^2 = 82$$
$$8^2 + 2^2 = 68$$
$$6^2 + 8^2 = 100$$
$$1^2 + 0^2 + 0^2 = 1$$

It wasn't even exciting to work that one out since I already knew that 133 was a happy number.

Zero is one of the most difficult numbers to understand. Last term we had to write Miss Meyers a factual composition, and I wrote about zero. Cindy teased me about it, saying that she hoped I wouldn't get a zero for it, but actually that was the first time I scored good marks for a composition.

The History of Zero
By Martin Retief

Zero was not always a number. Well, actually it was, because without zero, one would never have existed. But people didn't always know that, because when you count, you usually start with one. In India and China they only started using zero around 400 BCE, and the ancient Greeks had long debates about whether zero really was a number or not.

Today we know that you cannot do maths without using zero, and without zero computers couldn't be programmed. Zero is also called nil, nought or nothing. Zero is:

- *a whole number,*
- *an even number,*
- *a real number as well as an imaginary number (but that is very difficult to explain).*

If you add zero to a number or subtract it from that number, the same number remains. If you multiply any number by zero, the answer is zero. No number can be divided by zero — the answer is meaningless.

I yawned. Dying was like the number zero. It really existed and without it nothing would make sense. But that was very, very difficult to understand.

11

Riding a Bicycle Around the World

'Now remember: no rough play, and keep your jersey on,' Vusi's mum warned him on Thursday afternoon when she dropped him off at our house. 'And if you don't feel well, call me immediately. I'll fetch you at five sharp, OK?'

'Yea-eah, Mum,' he said impatiently.

His mum drove off, then stopped and started to wind down the window as if she wanted to say something else. But then she apparently changed her mind and headed out of the gate.

'Thank goodness,' a relieved Vusi sighed. 'Do you have any idea how I struggled to convince her to let me visit you this afternoon?'

'I can't believe you talked her round,' I said.

He nodded. 'If it hadn't been for Miranda... Believe it or not, *she* was the one who convinced my parents. And she didn't breathe a word about yesterday with the quad bike.'

I looked at my watch. 'Chris will be waiting for us.'

67

Vusi looked disappointed. 'Aren't we going inside first?' he asked and pointed in the direction of our house.

I shook my head and started walking towards the garage to fetch the bicycles. 'There's no time.'

Vusi ran after me with the backpack bouncing on his back.

'C'mon, Clucky, I've never been inside a real actress's house!'

'My mum's no longer an actress,' I said. 'Besides, she sleeps in the afternoon.'

'Flipping heck, you have a lot of chickens!' exclaimed Vusi when we came around the corner of the house.

The chickens were lazing in the afternoon sun. Here and there one was scratching the ground, searching for bugs.

I shrugged. 'They belonged to my dad. Since he died I've been looking after them.'

'I'm sorry,' said Vusi. 'About your dad. And about Cheetah catching one of your chickens.'

'Kathleen,' I said.

'Huh?'

'The chicken's name was Kathleen,' I said while taking my and Uncle Hendrik's bicycles from the garage. I couldn't believe he'd forgotten Kathleen's name *yet again*. 'You can ride on mine,' I said and gave him the bicycle with the basket in front. 'The gears on Uncle Hendrik's bike are a little dicey.'

Vusi put his backpack in the basket I always put the eggs in when I went to sell them. 'OK, let's get going,' he said.

Suddenly he looked very pale to me. What if something happened to him? His mum and dad would blame me because we hadn't stayed home all afternoon like we'd promised. 'Are you sure you'll be OK?'

He nodded. 'C'mon!'

The gears on Uncle Hendrik's bicycle made a grinding noise as we got going. When we rode out of the gate I carefully checked both sides of the road to make sure there was no sign of Vusi's mum. Fortunately the place Chris had talked about wasn't too far away.

'I've...never heard...of a girl...called...Chris,' wheezed Vusi after we'd covered some distance.

'Her real name is Christine,' I explained. 'But no one ever calls her that.'

I shot a furtive look at Vusi to see if he was OK. He was slightly red in the face, but at least it didn't look like he was going to faint or something.

'Did you know that someone from Scotland cycled around the world in 194 days and 17 hours?'

Vusi gave me a surprised look. 'Clucky...how come...you know about...things like that?'

'I read about stuff on the internet, during our computer lessons.'

'Yes, but normal people...never remember things like that.'

I didn't answer him immediately. I was hoping he wouldn't think there was something wrong with me.

'I like numbers,' I said after a while. 'My dad was also good with them. He was a data analyst. That's someone who works with numbers all day. Maybe I'll also do that after school.'

Vusi didn't answer. I suddenly felt bad that I'd talked about what I wanted to do after school. Did Vusi ever think about that, or did he only think about the 40% chance the doctor had predicted for him?

Fortunately there wasn't any more time to wonder or feel bad because Chris was standing by the side of the road, waiting for us. She had an old bicycle that looked even worse than Uncle Hendrik's.

'You guys are late,' she said. 'Move it.'

12

The Perfect Place to Hide from Zombies and Killer's Unplanned Demise

'Wow!' Vusi said excitedly when the shed door slid open, creaking and moaning. 'It's perfect!'

Dust whirled up in the shards of sunlight that fell across the cement floor. I peeped inside. The shed smelled of grease and dust, and a white Volkswagen Beetle was parked in between lots of cupboards and boxes.

'Whose place is this?' I asked.

'My uncle's,' Chris answered and put the small bunch of keys in the back pocket of her jeans. 'My mum rents it from him. For my brother's car, and his furniture and stuff.'

The moment Chris spoke about her brother, I knew I had to find a way to stop Vusi from asking any more questions.

'So where's your brother then? Overseas?'

Too late.

Chris shook her head. 'No. He's in Greenside.'

Vusi's mouth fell open. 'But Greenside is...'

'...a prison,' Chris finished his sentence. 'You're absolutely right.' She pushed a box aside. 'Come on in, but don't touch my brother's stuff, OK?'

I secretly gestured with my finger in front of my lips that Vusi should keep quiet, but he pretended not to see. 'Why is your brother in jail?'

Chris swung around, brushing the hair from her eyes. I saw that her eyes were blazing in her slender face. 'Let me see...' She counted on her fingers. 'Breaking and entering, possession of an illegal firearm, assaulting a police officer, obstructing the course of justice. Any more questions?'

When nobody said anything, she turned away and walked off.

There was just one single row of windows in the shed, high up close to the roof. Only after Chris had switched on the light could I see all the boxes and furniture and things in the shed clearly.

'Why would your brother need three microwaves?' Vusi wanted to know. 'And what are these? Hey, it looks like–'

'I told you to leave his stuff alone!' Chris hissed. 'Let's just forget about this. I thought I was doing you guys a favour, but–'

'OK, OK!' Vusi said and threw his hands into the air like someone who was giving himself up to the police. 'Sorry!'

I tried my best to show that I didn't condone his prying. I still didn't know how he'd found out that my mum was a famous actress way back, but slowly and surely I was beginning to understand. He was the most inquisitive person I had ever come across.

'This place is perfect for a horror movie,' said Vusi, looking around in awe.

As if on cue, a pigeon suddenly flew up somewhere close to the roof.

I got such a fright that chills ran down my spine.

Vusi dug into his backpack and took out his camera. 'We have to start with a scene that shows me approaching and discovering the shed.'

'I thought you were on a quad bike,' said Chris sceptically. 'In the movie.'

Vusi frowned. 'Hmmm. You're right. But my mum definitely won't allow me to bring the quad here.'

'In the movie you can always say that the quad ran out of petrol,' I suggested. 'And then you had to walk the rest of the way.'

'And the dog?' asked Chris.

Vusi and I looked at each other. We had forgotten about Cheetah – or rather, Killer.

Vusi slapped his forehead with his hand. 'I can't believe I was that dumb. What are we going to do? How on earth am I going to get Cheetah here? It's hard enough to get here without my mum and everyone knowing.'

Chris sat down on a box. 'What's wrong with your folks? I mean, aren't you allowed to go *anywhere*?'

'He's–' I started to explain, but Vusi immediately butted in.

'Grounded. As in seriously grounded. I'm not allowed to set foot outside the house for the next month or there'll be serious trouble.'

'Oh, OK,' said Chris.

Part of me was glad that we didn't have to tell Chris the truth, but another part of me felt guilty because Vusi had lied to her.

'Maybe Killer changed into a zombie,' I said.

'What d'you mean?' Vusi wanted to know.

'Well, he bit me in the previous scene, when I was a zombie. Who says dogs don't also change into zombies?'

'And then?' asked Chris, as if she was listening to a story.

Embarrassed, I shrugged. 'I don't know... erm...'

Vusi lightly punched me on the shoulder. 'Clucky, you're brilliant!' He picked up his camera. 'C'mon, we have work to do. We'll shoot the first two scenes outside, and then I'll discover the shed.'

A few minutes later, we were standing outside under a tree. Vusi put my dad's jacket on and dusted off his trousers. Then he picked up the video camera and got it into position. There was a sad expression on his face.

Chris just stood watching, looking terribly amused.

'OK, I'm ready,' said Vusi. 'Start the countdown, Clucky.'

I stepped back a bit. 'OK Three...two... one...action!'

Vusi looked down for a few moments. Then he faced the camera. 'I got Killer when he was only six weeks old. From the word go, he was crazy about me. It's true what people say – a dog is a man's best friend. Killer was–'

Chris burst out laughing.

'Cut!' Vusi shouted angrily and switched off the camera. He gave Chris a miffed look. 'What's so funny?'

'I... I'm sorry,' Chris laughed. 'It's just...you look really funny when you pretend to be so sad...about a dog called Killer...'

'What does his name have to do with anything?' a peeved Vusi demanded.

'Nothing,' said Chris with a serious face, and then she started laughing again.

'You've messed up the whole scene.'

'OK, OK, I'm sorry,' said Chris. 'Start again, from the beginning.'

It looked as if Vusi wanted to argue some more, but he picked up the camera again and nodded at me.

'Three...two...one...action!'

Again he looked down for a couple of seconds before facing the camera. 'I got Killer when he was still a tiny puppy. Only six weeks old. From the word go, he was crazy about me. After the zombie plague broke out, he was all I had left. And now I've lost him too...This morning he saved my life when one of the zombies attacked me.' Vusi stared into space for a moment and then he said, 'Cut!'

'Flipping heck, is the whole movie this depressing?' asked Chris.

Vusi ignored her and looked at his watch. 'We have to hurry. I still want to shoot the scene in which I discover the shed.'

'When are we going to see *more* zombies?' asked Chris. 'I thought it was supposed to be a zombie movie. I've never heard of a zombie movie with only one zombie.'

I could see Vusi gritting his teeth.

'Vusi knows exactly what needs to happen in the story,' I said quickly.

Chris grunted. 'OK, if you say so.'

Vusi gave her a look. I'm not very good at knowing what certain kinds of look mean, but I was sure this look meant that if there was ever a real zombie plague, Vusi wouldn't mind if they got hold of Chris first.

13

Problems

Mr Faure didn't do maths – he attacked it. When he was writing on the board it looked as if he was trying to demolish the numbers with the chalk. He never spoke about 'sums'; he always called them 'problems'. As in, '*For homework I want you to solve all the problems on page seventy-four.*'

Mr Faure regarded us plot plodders as problems too – I once overheard him saying to another teacher that the lot of us were mostly problem children.

At the beginning of the year, I raised my hand when he was doing a sum on the board. I told him that there was an easier and quicker way to get to the solution. 'Fine, if you're that bright, why don't you play teacher from now on?' he snapped. 'Here's the chalk. Come and stand at the front and teach the rest of this lesson.' The entire class burst out laughing as I took up position in front of the board. I wasn't sure if I really was supposed to do the rest of the sums on the board, so I just stood there while everyone laughed at me. From that day on, Mr Faure despised me. I always made sure I scored somewhere between 60% and 70% in my maths tests so that he would leave me alone. Had I scored any higher, he probably would've thought that I was trying to look clever again.

That Friday morning, he was battling with a graph on the board. He explained it very slowly and it sounded like he was already angry in advance because he knew some kids wouldn't understand the work. My eyes drifted off to the piece of paper on my desk. Vusi had said that we were going to shoot an exciting scene that afternoon. I picked up my pencil and started drawing.

'Martin Retief!'

I jumped with fright.

A couple of children giggled, but Mr Faure quickly shut them up with a stare.

'Is it asking too much to expect you to pay attention in my class?' He snatched the page from my desk and took a look at it. 'What's this?'

I gulped. 'Just a picture, sir.'

'And does this look like the art class to you?'

I shook my head. 'No, sir.'

'How many times do I have to ask you to pay attention in my class?'

I lowered my head. 'I don't know, sir.'

Again, a few kids dared to laugh.

'You'll sit in detention this afternoon,' he said and walked back to the board.

'But, sir!' It popped out before I could stop it.

'Enough!' he bellowed.

I sank back into my chair. Safraaz gave me a killer look. Sitting in detention on a Friday was the worst punishment on earth. It meant the school bus had to wait for you for an hour, so Mr Oldman and the other plot plodders would be angry at you for days.

For the rest of the lesson I didn't dare take my eyes off the board.

'Clucky, you idiot,' said Chris during break when she heard that I had detention. But then she smiled unexpectedly. 'Don't worry. Mr Faure is a grumpy old fart.'

The funny thing was that teachers also hated detention. They always looked bored to death when they had to supervise us for an hour. That day it was Miss Cullen's turn. I thought she was given this horrible job because she was still a student teacher. She had to teach at our school for an entire term before she could qualify for her teacher's diploma. Fortunately she was very kind. She sometimes took us for an Afrikaans lesson.

When I walked into the media centre, I saw that she was already seated at the desk and working. Two Grade Sixes and I were the only ones in detention. Miss Cullen looked up and smiled.

'Well then,' she said. 'Welcome to our labour camp. Find something to keep yourselves busy. And I don't want to hear a sound, understand?'

I took out my English textbook and started doing my homework. After I finished the comprehension test, I looked at the clock on the wall. There was still another half an hour of detention left. By this time, everyone waiting for me in the bus was probably livid.

On the right-hand side of my desk was a small pile of books and papers. Miss Cullen was sitting with her head bent, working. I picked the books up one by one and flipped through the papers. They looked like photocopies of old maths tests.

Softly I tore a sheet from my exercise book and started to do one of the sums on it. I'd noticed that some people were scared of maths. People like Mr Faure. But I knew maths wasn't something to be scared of. Dad always said that it was a kind of game, like crossword puzzles or chess. The better you understood the rules, the better you got at it. When I saw a maths sum, a lot of roads immediately opened up in my mind. I don't know how else to explain it. It's like only reading the first page of a story and then closing the book and trying to imagine all the different ways the story could end. When you do a sum it's like telling a story in such a way that you get to the happy ending by the shortest possible route.

'Have you perhaps seen my notes?' asked Miss Cullen, startling me.

I gasped and quickly pushed the pile of papers aside. Then I caught her eye on my desk.

'Oh, this is where I left them.' She gathered the sheets and arranged them in a neat pile together with the books. 'All right, you may go now. But don't get into trouble again, OK!'

I was surprised to see that the time had passed so quickly. I was also surprised to see that Miss Cullen had let us leave ten minutes early. When I looked at her, she winked as if that was a secret between the two of us.

In the bus everyone was sulking, waiting for me.

As I got in, Mr Oldman growled, 'Clucky Retief, if I miss my rugby on TV this afternoon, I'll have you for dinner.'

14

A Bloody Scene

'What have you got in there?' Chris wanted to know as Vusi unpacked his backpack. 'I hope there's something to eat because I'm starving – and of course that's all due to you-know-who over here who had detention.'

I felt the blood rushing to my face. Everything was always my fault. It was my fault that everyone in the bus had to wait. It was my fault that Mr Oldman might miss the rugby on TV. It was my fault that Chris didn't have time to eat lunch because she had to walk all the way from her house to the shed after the school bus dropped her off. I'm sure she was even going to blame me for the fact that her dilapidated old bike had a flat tyre. I was about to open my mouth and say something when I saw that she was smiling.

'Hey, I'm just teasing, Clucky,' she said.

I grinned, feeling embarrassed.

'This afternoon we're going to shoot a very scary scene,' Vusi announced. He held the zombie mask and a transparent plastic bag up in the air. 'Clucky, you're going to be the zombie again.'

'All the zombies can't look exactly the same,' Chris said with a frown. 'Can't it be a girl zombie this time?'

Vusi shook his head. 'No, you're the girl who's hiding in the shed. You can't be a zombie as well.'

'I can be a zombie with one arm. Like Mr Oldman,' I suggested. I pulled my one arm out of my jersey sleeve and held it tight against my chest while I stumbled forward and hollered 'AHHHHH!' the way Vusi had taught me.

Chris laughed.

'Cool!' Vusi was impressed. 'That's a great idea. But wait till you see the best part...'

My eyes widened when I saw what he took from the backpack. 'Vusi...where did you find that?'

'Relax, it's just a toy,' Vusi said and wielded the pistol with apparent ease. 'Look, I also brought an old T-shirt. We're going to stick this bag of fake blood inside your jersey, then you just have to press on it hard so that it'll explode and soak your entire shirt with blood.'

Vusi looked very pleased with himself. But Chris didn't look happy at all.

'Vusi, haven't you learned your lesson with the dog and the quad bike?' she asked impatiently.

'What now?' sighed Vusi.

'You can't just suddenly have a firearm in the movie,' Chris explained. 'Why didn't you use it the first time the zombie attacked you? Why didn't you use it to save Killer?'

'Erm...' Vusi looked devastated.

'I have a better plan,' said Chris immediately. 'I'll rescue you from the zombie.' She took the pistol from him. 'The zombie's chasing you and you're running to get to the shed in time. And then, the minute you open the door, I grab hold of you...and then...BOOM!' She aimed the pistol in my direction.

'Arrrrgggh!' I groaned and collapsed.

Chris pretended to blow some smoke from the tip of the barrel. 'Take that, you living corpse!' she growled.

Vusi laughed. 'Yes, OK. I guess that could work. Go on, unlock the shed so that we can start. And wear your hair loose, not in a ponytail like now.'

Chris shot him a puzzled look but then loosened her hair. It fell over her shoulders and almost reached her hips. 'Satisfied?'

I looked away, feeling awkward.

Vusi seemed really chuffed. Chris unlocked the shed and gave the door a kick to make it open more easily.

'Look,' said Vusi when the lights went on, 'there's a lot of new stuff in here.' In awe, he bent over and stared at a music centre that had been placed on one of the tables.

'Hey, I told you to leave this stuff alone,' Chris said angrily. 'Some of it belongs to my uncle.'

'OK, OK,' Vusi pacified her. 'I've just had a brainwave! If we bring a CD along, we can play background music for the movie while we're shooting this scene.'

Chris firmly shook her head. 'No, you leave this stuff alone or we're pushing off.'

'Never mind, it'll be better if I add the music later.' Vusi quickly changed his tune. 'When I edit the movie on my computer.'

Clearly, he knew better than to disagree with Chris.

15

Good Times and the Value of π

Sometimes a day can be unpredictable. It may look like it's going to be the lousiest day ever, and then it can suddenly turn out to be one of the best days ever.

'*Stop right there! How d'you know that I'm a zombie? Erm...*'

'*Stop right there! I know you're a zombie! Or rather, I mean...*'

'*Stop right there, erm...zombie! Ah, dammit!*'

We were rolling around with laughter as Vusi showed us on the camera screen how Chris had struggled to get her lines right.

'I never said I wanted to become an actress,' said Chris.

'Too late,' said Vusi. 'You already have a role in a movie.'

Chris threw her head back and dramatically brushed her hair out of her face. 'In that case,' she said in a husky voice, 'I want my own trailer. And a limousine.'

Vusi pretended to open the door of the dusty old Beetle for her.

Chris just smiled. 'So what's going to happen next? You flee from the zombies, you discover a pretty girl in a shed and she saves your life... How will the movie end?'

Vusi sat down on a large wooden crate. His dark eyes looked serious now. 'It has to end with a bang, a big scene...a whole mob of zombies attacking the shed.'

'And where are we going to find that many zombies?' asked Chris.

Vusi looked at me. 'We'll make a plan.'

I checked my watch. 'Erm... Vusi, we'd better leave. Your mum's going to pick you up soon.'

'Will one of you give me a lift?' Chris wanted to know. 'I don't feel like walking home.'

'You can catch a ride on my bike,' I quickly offered because Vusi looked quite tired. 'I mean, on Uncle Hendrik's bike. But I'm riding it. I mean, you can get on Uncle Hendrik's bike with me.' My face was getting hot.

Chris smiled at me. 'Thanks.'

I felt nervous while I waited for Chris to lock the shed door. I'd never given anyone a lift on my bicycle. But Uncle Hendrik and Dad used to give me a lift when I was small, so I knew what to do. I sat back so that Chris could get on. She sat on the frame, between the handles and the seat.

'If you let me fall, I'm going to wring your neck,' she warned.

I just nodded and carefully started pedalling. She was so light that I almost didn't notice that she was on the bike. Her hair was blowing gently in the wind. She held it against her neck with one hand but strands of hair blew against my chest. I could smell her shampoo.

Vusi rode more slowly than usual. Was I imagining it, or was he very pale?

We'd hardly arrived at my house when his mum stopped in front of the gate.

'Should I ask my mum to drop you off at home?' he asked Chris.

She shook her head. 'No worries, my limo's waiting,' she said and pointed at my bike.

'OK, so see you guys tomorrow,' he said. 'Same time, same place.' His shoulders looked too frail to carry the backpack any further.

'Hey, look at the little chicks!' Chris exclaimed and gestured at a hen and her seven little ones walking around the corner of the house, scratching for food.

I nodded. 'That's Lizzie, and they're her first chicks.' I fetched the tin of chicken feed and spread some of it on the ground. Lizzie and her brood immediately rushed up, clucking.

Chris went down on her haunches close to the chickens. 'They're so sweet!' she whispered. Her eyes were shining and she was smiling. For a minute or so she remained motionless, watching the chickens, then she seemed to remember that I was around too.

'I have to get home,' she said.

'OK.'

I fetched the bicycle from where it was leaning against the wall in the late afternoon sun. Chris got on and we rode out of the gate. I hoped my mum wasn't watching us through the window, otherwise I'd have a lot of questions to answer about Chris that evening.

The air was cool. Chris shut her eyes tightly while I rode. I took it in turns to look at the road and her. There was a programme on TV once about scientists at a university who used maths to find out why some people had beautiful faces. They measured stuff like the distance between your chin and your nose, and then worked out all kinds of ratios to get to a number.

I was so lost in thought that I was startled when Chris spoke. 'What are you thinking about?'

The bike swerved dangerously and my cheeks were hot despite the cool wind.

'Nothing.'

'Liar. You're always thinking of stuff – it's obvious. You think in the school bus as well.' Her voice was teasing me. 'C'mon then, tell me something.'

My head was working overtime but I couldn't think of anything to say. So I said the first thing that popped into my head. 'OK...erm...do you know what pi is?'

A frown appeared between her eyes. 'I assume you're not talking about that stuff that gives people indigestion, so...it has something to do with circles, doesn't it?'

'Pi is the ratio of the circumference of a circle to its diameter. Or the ratio between the area of a circle to the square of its radius. It never changes.' The faster I spoke, the quicker my legs pumped the pedals. 'The value of pi is an irrational number because you can't write it down as a simple fraction.'

'Slow down!' Chris yelled, laughing. 'You want to kill us?'

I braked lightly. 'Sorry,' I mumbled. 'It's boring, I know.'

She shook her head. 'No, it's nice to hear you speak, even though I didn't really understand everything you said! You're always so quiet. Tell me more about pi...'

I just shook my head.

'C'mon, Clucky!' She prodded me. 'Don't stop.'

'People have been trying for ages to memorize as many different digits of pi as they can. It's called piphilology. A Chinese man learned 67,890 digits of pi by heart – it took him more than 24 hours to recite them. And in 2009 a professor claimed that he knew 30 million digits of pi by heart.'

Chris stared at me wide-eyed. 'Thirty million? No way, man!'

'It's impossible to put him to the test because even if you could speak for twenty-four hours a day, it would take you almost a year to recite that many digits. But the scientists who tested him think he spoke the truth.'

'No one can learn that many numbers by heart,' Chris said and shook her head.

I shrugged. 'People's minds work differently.'

We stopped in the dirt road at Chris's gate. In front of their house laundry was flapping in the wind. She nimbly hopped off the bike.

'You know what, Clucky Retief? I don't know exactly how your mind works, but you have one of the most interesting minds I've ever come across in my life...'

Then she leaned forward and kissed me.

16

A Chatty Old Lady
and an Awful Silence

'Have I ever told you about the chickens my hubby and I had?' asked Aunt Hantie. 'Way back, on the farm. Those chickens laid eggs morning, noon and night! I helped pay my children's way through university with the egg money I saved.' She sighed. 'And what do I have to show for that? Nothing. The old man, bless his soul, passed on ten years ago. And the two children are overseas. They hardly ever call me, only on Christmas and birthdays.'

'Erm… Auntie, I'm a little late,' I said gingerly.

Once Aunt Hantie got going, she hardly ever stopped talking. And I was running late; it was almost dark. Only after I'd dropped off Chris did I remember the eggs. The icky fake blood was still sticking to my chest.

Aunt Hantie blew a large pink chewing-gum bubble in the cold evening air. 'Ah, what a strange world we live in. Everything's so rushed. Well then, I wish you a pleasant evening, Clucky. Thanks for the eggs. At least you're slightly cheaper than Moosa's cafe. His prices are criminal – it's daylight robbery. Talking of robbery, did you hear about the break-in the other day at–'

'Auntie, I really have to go,' I interrupted her.

'All right, my boy,' she said. 'Till next time then.'

I shifted around uncomfortably. 'Erm… Auntie…you haven't paid me yet.'

For a moment she looked confused. 'Goodness, child, I'm sorry. Where's my head today?' She counted out the money for the dozen eggs into my hand.

While racing home, I thought of Aunt Hantie. She said that her husband died ten years ago. That amounts to 3,652 days, if you add two days for leap years. And that amounts to 87,648 hours. How do you survive that many hours when you're as lonely as she is?

By the time I got home it was dark. I put my bike away in our shed. Mum, Uncle Hendrik and Cindy were already sitting at the table when I got inside. I could smell fish and chips for supper.

'Sorry I'm late. I had to go and sell eggs and…' My words dried up when I saw my mum's face.

'Go and wash your hands then come and eat,' she said.

When I sat down at the table, Cindy glared at me as if she'd just heard that I abused puppies. (Whatever it was, it wasn't that – I had never treated an animal badly. Except maybe that time when I was small and forgot to clean the fish bowl and they all died, but that really had not been on purpose.)

My mum dished up for me without breathing a word. Uncle Hendrik didn't look up from his plate.

The fish on my plate reminded me of the dead goldfish, and I was no longer hungry. But I suspected I was in trouble already, so I didn't dare say that I didn't want to eat.

'What are you and the neighbours' son up to?' Mum asked as I put the first bite of fish into my mouth.

I swallowed. The fish felt dry in my mouth. 'We're making a movie. About zombies.'

Oh no. I immediately knew what this was all about. Vusi's mum had probably found out that we'd sneaked away on the bicycles to shoot the movie somewhere else. And she had probably talked to my mum, and now there was trouble...

Mum's eyes pinned me to my seat. 'Have the two of you been in your dad's and my room?'

It was so unexpected that I didn't know what to say. I took a sip of milk to gulp the fish down. So I'd been wrong about Vusi's mum. It was much worse...

'Clucky, where is Dad's leather jacket?' Mum asked with a dangerous tone in her voice.

There was an awful silence as everyone waited for me to answer.

'I... I just borrowed it. For the movie.'

Mum took a deep breath and made a wheezing sound before she let fly. 'Borrowed? To play with? Don't you have any respect?'

'Trisa...' said Uncle Hendrik softly, but there was no stopping Mum.

'Your dad's gone, Clucky...'

I gritted my teeth and fought back the tears that were burning behind my eyes. My breath was racing, burning my nose.

'...and you're playing with his clothes!'

I jumped up, not paying attention to the chair falling over and clattering to the floor. 'He isn't *gone*!' I screamed. 'He's dead! But no one in this house ever speaks about that. You all pretend that nothing has happened. He's dead! Have you forgotten? He went to buy fish...' I shoved the plate of fish and chips aside. 'And there was an accident and he's never going to need a jacket again and he's never going to...' I choked back

my tears. 'He's not gone!' I screamed. 'He's never going to sleep in a bed again–'

'Clucky, stop it!' yelled Cindy.

'He's not a zombie!'

Mum was surprisingly fast. The imprint of her hand burned on my face where she slapped me. The same cheek that Chris had kissed earlier that afternoon.

For a split second, everyone was dead quiet, like in a movie. Then Cindy started crying and I stormed off to my room.

17

My Dad and a Brilliant Plan

Ten things I remembered about my dad:

1. How he would get home in the afternoon and shout, 'Good afternoon, slaves! Bring my tobacco and bring my pipe!' Even though he didn't smoke.

2. His golden tooth that you could only see when he was having a really good laugh.

3. The time when he and Mum polished off a whole bottle of wine in the lounge and danced to old-fashioned records while Cindy and I egged them on by clapping our hands.

4. The way he always went outside to shake off the loose hairs after Mum had cut his hair.

5. The time when Byron, the white rooster, died, and Dad and I buried him in the moonlight under the willow tree.

6. The time when I showered with him and we sang old folk songs until Mum complained

that she'd get a migraine if we didn't stop right away.

7. His English Leather aftershave.

8. The time he scolded Cindy and me after we pinched his mobile phone and called all the numbers on it to congratulate people on winning a camel. (That was Cindy's idea. Only one person had been interested in the camel.)

9. His hands.

10. How he taught me to do long division sums when I was only in Grade Two.

It was late. I'd heard Mum switch off the TV and brush her teeth more than an hour ago.

It was weird, but I wasn't quite sure how I felt about everything that had happened that day.

Vusi and his zombies.

Chris who had kissed me.

The fight at the table.

In a way I just felt...flat. Like a can of soft drink that had been shaken and then left open.

I wasn't really used to having friends. It was weird how things had worked out. If Cheetah hadn't bitten and killed Kathleen, I would never have walked over to knock on Vusi's door. And if Vusi hadn't found out that Mum used to be an actress ages ago, I wouldn't have punched him. And if I hadn't punched him, I'd never have been forced to go and apologize, and then we'd never have started to shoot the movie. And if we hadn't been shooting a movie, Chris would never have ridden on my bicycle.

It was almost like maths, as if someone was working on a complicated sum in which I was one of the numbers.

Maybe the movie was part of the sum. I didn't really know why Vusi was so keen to make it, and I didn't really understand what the story was about. But I knew it was something Vusi simply *had* to do. The same way I *had* to count the number of peas on my plate. Maybe it helped him to forget about his disease. Maybe pretending to shoot and kill zombies made him less scared of dying.

My tummy growled; I was desperately hungry. I sat up in my bed and rummaged through the drawer of my bedside table. Under a pile of papers I found a few old toffees.

Where on earth were we going to find a horde of zombies for the movie's final scene?

At the exact moment I bit into a toffee, a brilliant idea came to me.

18

Vusi's Mum

I waited at the post office counter for the lady to bring the photocopies. She'd already finished a while back, but she was standing with them in her hand and chatting to one of her colleagues. Vusi would be at my house in a couple of minutes. My eyes were burning after an almost sleepless night, but still, I was really chuffed with my plan.

'There you are,' the woman finally said and placed the pile of papers on the counter. When she spoke, you could see the chewing gum in her mouth.

I quickly paid and put the photocopies in my backpack.

Outside the post office I unlocked the chain on my bike and rushed home.

There was just enough time to hide the wad of papers under my bed before Vusi's mum drove up to the house. The other times she had simply dropped him off and left, but this Saturday afternoon she switched off the engine and got out of the car.

'Good afternoon... Clucky,' she greeted. I could hear that she didn't like using my nickname.

'Afternoon, ma'am.'

'Is your mum home?'

Vusi gave me an apologetic look.

'Unfortunately she's sleeping,' I said. Ten to one that was the truth – my mum often slept away the afternoon after watching TV almost right through the night.

'Oh...erm...well, that's a pity. Then I'll come and speak to her some other time.'

'Mum!' said Vusi, sounding annoyed.

His mum zipped up his jacket and straightened the collar. 'Take care, Vusi. Remember what the doctor said.' She turned to me. 'Clucky, please don't play any rough games. Vusi went to the specialist today and–'

'He said I'm doing better!' Vusi interrupted her. 'He said if things go on like this, I might not need chemo again.'

His mum nodded. 'That's right. But it means we have to be even more careful. You can't afford a setback now.'

'Ye-e-e-es, Mum!' said Vusi.

She unlocked the car. 'Well then, I'll fetch you at five again.'

'That's good news,' I said as his mum drove out of the gate.

Vusi pretended not to hear me. 'C'mon, Chris must be waiting for us.'

When he said her name, I felt something stir in my tummy.

What if she acted weird after the kiss yesterday?

What if she thought I was weird after everything I had said on the cycle ride home?

What if…?

'Clucky, move it!' Vusi called.

I sighed and got on Uncle Hendrik's bicycle.

19

An Unpleasant Surprise

'What d'you think? Where did the zombies come from?' Chris asked the camera.

I was peeping at them through a crack in the old cupboard door. It was difficult to peek through a cupboard door, and even more so when you were trying to see through two holes in a zombie mask. As if that wasn't bad enough, the cupboard was dusty and I was trying my best not to sneeze.

Vusi looked lost in thought and then slowly shook his head. When he spoke, it was in the deep voice that he used every time he was in front of the camera. His Brad voice. 'Who knows? Maybe some science experiment went horribly wrong. Maybe it was a radioactive spillage. Maybe it was some alien virus from space. I only know one thing: I don't want to become one of them.'

Vusi looked at Chris impatiently. 'I said, *I definitely don't want to become one of them*,' he repeated.

At last Chris realized that it was her cue to say something. 'Erm...er...shush!' She put her finger in front of her mouth. 'I think I hear something!'

Both of them froze.

Vusi scanned the semi-dark shed with his camera. 'I don't see anything,' he said. 'Maybe it was your imagina—'

'ARRRRGGGGHHHH!' I burst out of the cupboard.

Vusi and Chris screamed.

I limped towards them. 'ARRRGGGHHH-tishoo!' I couldn't hold in the sneeze any longer.

Fortunately Vusi hadn't heard it, otherwise he would've stopped and started again from the beginning. He grabbed the spade that was leaning against the wall and lunged at me.

'Take that, you piece of zombie junk!' he yelled.

I ducked instinctively when he raised the spade, even though I knew he was only pretending to hit me.

'Shush!' Chris called out anxiously. 'I hear something!'

Vusi lowered the spade. 'Dammit, Chris, you've already said those words.'

Suddenly there was a grinding sound as the shed door was pushed open. A block of bright sunlight appeared on the cement floor. Vusi, Chris and I were petrified.

'Well, well, well... What do we have here? Guys, come and check this out.'

The voice sounded vaguely familiar.

I shot Chris and Vusi a horrified look. Three men were walking into the shed. It took a moment for my eyes to adjust to the sharp light. But when he spoke again, I recognized the one who was in front.

'What the hell are you doing here?'

Bruce.

'Have you been messing with our stuff?' one of the other guys asked. He was a tall, skinny man with a shaved head.

Chris stepped forward. 'This is my brother's place,' she said. 'He rents it. What are you guys doing here?'

Her voice was so angry that I got a bit of a fright. Had I been those three guys, I would've scrammed right away. But it didn't scare them off.

'Your brother's place?' Bruce laughed. 'Your brother's in jail, Blondie – have you forgotten? And while he's locked up, we're looking after his business. Right, guys?'

The other two closed in on us with a menacing look on their faces.

I swallowed. It was unfair that Chris had to do all the talking.

'I...we're sorry...' I stammered. 'We haven't touched your things, honest.'

'Is it stolen stuff?' Vusi asked out of the blue. He sounded like one of those stupid TV detectives who'd just unravelled a big secret. If there'd been a competition for the dumbest question on earth, Vusi would have won hands down.

Bruce moved surprisingly fast for someone so big. The next thing we knew, Vusi's neck was in a vice-like grip. 'You're a little know-it-all, eh, Baldy?' he sneered.

'Check it out, Bruce,' said the third guy, running his hand through his dark hair. 'They have a video camera. They've been filming everything. If the cops get hold of that video we'll be done for. It's evidence.'

'Shut up,' said Bruce. He yanked the camera from Vusi's hands.

Vusi only managed one single groan. Something was shining against his neck. A knife.

I lunged forward. 'Please!' I begged. 'He's sick. He has Hodgkin's disease and it's a kind of cancer. I read on the internet that the author Jane Austen died of it, and the guy who discovered Tutankhamen's grave, and...and the doctor said if something happened to him now, it could get worse again. We really didn't know about your stuff and I swear we won't say anything!' My chest was burning and it felt as if I couldn't breathe.

All three guys laughed.

'Take off that mask,' said Bruce.

I felt like an idiot as I pulled off the zombie mask. I'd forgotten that it was still on my head.

'Clucky!' said Bruce, surprised. He relaxed his grip on Vusi's neck.

'Hey, Bruce, it's your chick's little brother,' said the dark-haired man, suddenly amused. 'That weird kid who's always riding around on his bike peddling eggs!'

For a moment there was silence. The only sound was Bruce's knife clicking open and shut. He seemed to be trying to decide what to do. Then he shoved the video camera into Vusi's hand. 'Take the video out.'

'It doesn't work with a video,' said Vusi curtly. 'Only old-fashioned video cameras still use a video. This one has a memory card and–'

'Just take the damn thing out!' Bruce growled and jabbed him in the back.

Vusi removed the memory card and Bruce grabbed it from him. When Bruce crushed the memory card between his fingers, Chris gasped.

'No!' shouted Vusi. 'Our movie! Please…

please... That's our movie... *The End of the World*... It's about zombies and...and we won't tell anyone about–'

With a sharp click the card snapped in two.

Vusi froze.

Without thinking about it, I stepped closer to Chris and put my arm around her.

'That'll teach you to stay away from places where you don't belong,' said Bruce with a grin. He took the video camera from Vusi and threw it to the dark-haired guy. 'We'll keep the camera, thanks a lot. If it's as new as you say, we'll get a couple of bucks for it. And if one of you breathes so much as a word about this, there'll be hell to pay...'

Bruce walked right up to us and grinned with his face almost against mine. 'Clucky, you don't want anything to happen to your pretty sis now, do you?' He snatched the zombie mask out of my hand and slashed the rubber open, from the one eye to the gaping mouth.

I felt the blade of his knife against my throat and swallowed drily. Slowly I shook my head, careful not to let the knife draw blood.

Then Bruce turned to Chris. He gently stroked her chin with his forefinger, the way you do with a puppy. 'And you, girly, if you make waves, things will get even tougher for your brother. If the cops find out that he's still operating from inside prison, he's going to be behind bars for many more years. And trust me, your big brother won't be pleased when he hears that his little sis has been poking her nose into his business.' He took a step back and ran his fingers through his peroxide hair. 'Get lost – off you go. And don't let me catch any of you anywhere near here again.'

I pulled Vusi's sleeve and at last he moved.

As we headed out, Bruce grabbed Chris by the arm. 'Not so fast, Blondie. The key?'

Without a word, Chris dropped the key for the padlock into his hand.

20

A Conversation with Some Chickens

'Three point one four one five nine two six five three five eight nine seven nine three two three eight four six two six four three three eight three two seven nine five zero two eight eight four... erm...one nine seven...erm...'

I sighed and gave up.

Isaiah shot me a sideways look and gave such a big chicken yawn that the white membranes slid over his eyes. Then he scratched his head and shook his feathers. Lizzie clucked while scratching the ground with her chicks.

From the house I vaguely heard the theme song of *The Bold and the Beautiful*.

Not even the value of pi could make me forget what had happened earlier that afternoon.

On the way home I had tried to speak to Vusi, but he hadn't been interested in anything I had to say. The entire movie was on the memory card that Bruce had snapped in two.

Vusi had even ignored me when I offered to use my egg money to buy a new video camera. I didn't know what he would tell his parents when they found out that the camera was gone.

But the worst thing had been Chris. She was furious when we got outside. Actually, Vusi and I should have been angry at her – it had been her idea to use the shed. How were we supposed to know that her brother's mates were using it to store stolen goods?

Her cheeks were flaming red as she threw her hair over her shoulder. 'Cancer! Vusi, you have *cancer* and no one told me about it. When were you planning to tell me?'

I was worried that she would burst into tears because I had no idea what I'd do then.

But she didn't cry. She gave Uncle Hendrik's bicycle a kick. 'You and your stupid movie!' And then she stomped off down the road. After a couple of steps, she shouted over her shoulder, 'I never want to see you guys again, OK!'

I knew that that was impossible. She would obviously see me on the bus and at school. But I decided that it wasn't a good idea to tell her that at that specific moment. Besides, I understood what she meant when she said she didn't want to have anything to do with us again. It meant I wouldn't be able to tell her that I'd read on

Wikipedia that the singer Kate Bush had written a song that consisted mostly of the numbers of pi. And that 14 March was International Pi Day.

'Three point one four one five nine two six five three five eight nine seven nine three two three eight four six two six four three three eight three two seven nine five zero two eight... eight...'

I had to do something.

Vusi was miserable.

Chris was furious.

Neither of them was even going to attempt to make a plan.

'I have to do something, Isaiah,' I said out loud to the chicken.

He woke with a startled clucking sound and threw me a suspicious look.

21

Riding a Bicycle in the Moonlight

Unfortunately, luck wasn't on my side. After supper Mum headed for the lounge with a box of tissues and a small box of Quality Street. That meant she was going to watch some Saturday night chick flick on TV and wouldn't go to bed early.

On the other hand, I was lucky in one respect: Cindy had called to let us know that she was going to sleep at a friend's house because they had to study together for a test the following week. I didn't know whether that was the truth; Cindy often lied to my mum when she and Bruce wanted to go to some wild party. But that meant that I wouldn't have to face Bruce that evening. When I closed my eyes I could still see his face, and feel the cold steel of his knife against my throat. Had he really meant what he said? Would he really hurt Cindy?

Before Dad had died, she had always been full of jokes, and even though we had sometimes fought, we had got along well. She and Mum never quarrelled that often; they used to love doing things together. On Saturdays they went shopping and Dad would complain that they were going to bankrupt him.

Lying in the dark, I stared at the slowly changing electronic digits of my alarm clock, thinking about everything that had happened over the past few days. Everyone had been talking so much about the gang, the one that had broken into Safraaz's dad's shop. By now I was convinced Bruce and his friends were the culprits. They were probably using the storage space rented by Chris's mum to keep the stolen goods until they could sell them. I clenched my teeth. How much would they get for Vusi's video camera?

23:03.

$$2^2 + 3^2 + 0^2 + 3^2 = 20$$
$$2^2 + 0^2 = 4$$
$$4^2 = 16$$
$$1^2 + 6^2 = 37$$
$$3^2 + 7^2 = 58$$
$$5^2 + 8^2 = 89$$
$$8^2 + 9^2 = 145$$
$$1^2 + 4^2 + 5^2 = 42$$
$$4^2 + 2^2 = 20$$

So 2,303 wasn't a happy number.

When the alarm clock changed to 23:04, I saw the sliver of light that had been shining from the lounge under my door go out.

At last.

I lay in bed, listening to Mum brushing her teeth in the bathroom and drinking water in the kitchen. The couch in the lounge squeaked when she lay down on it. Then the house became quiet. To make sure that the coast was clear, I lay waiting for another ten minutes.

At exactly 23:46, I threw the duvet aside and got out of bed. My sneakers and backpack were ready and waiting. I tiptoed through the dark house in my socks. In the kitchen the fridge was purring like a sleeping cat. I made sure the keys didn't make a noise when I unlocked the door.

It was freezing outside. Everything seemed to be glowing faintly in the bright moonlight. I put my sneakers on. My bike was under the saltbush where I'd hidden it earlier that evening. One of the hens made a sleepy sound as if she wanted to ask me what I was up to, but then all was quiet again.

My sneakers and the wheels of the bike crunched on the gravel, and the key and chain on the front gate jingled when I unlocked it. But fortunately the house remained dark. Only when I was outside the gate did I get on my bicycle.

The chain whirred rhythmically as I pedalled. The only other sound was a dog barking somewhere in the distance. I pulled my beanie tighter over my ears.

I tried desperately not to think about what I was doing. I stopped at a gate and took one of the papers from my backpack. As I slipped it into the letter box a dog started to bark inside.

'Shush!' I whispered and pedalled off as fast as possible.

By the time I'd slipped a paper into the letter box at the fourth house, my hands were numb. As I continued down the road, a car's bright headlights appeared in the darkness. I jumped off the bike and stood frozen against a hedge of shrubs along the side of the road. Breathlessly, I watched the car come closer. Only when I saw the red tail lights disappear did I dare breathe again.

I put my hand in my backpack and felt the wad of papers. I'd had fifty photocopies made. There were still a lot to hand out. My fingers hit upon the cold metal of the iron saw.

It was going to be a long night.

22

Breaking In

I think that when you're used to breaking into people's houses you never expect someone to break into *yours*. Bruce and his gang might have changed the shed's padlock to keep Chris, Vusi and me out, but fortunately they replaced it with a cheap one.

The iron saw made a horrible screeching sound in the silence of the night. I wished I could see how far I had sawn through the shackle of the padlock, but I was too scared to switch on the torch.

It was after two when I'd finally dropped all the papers in the letter boxes but I had no idea what time it was now.

The cold was difficult to ignore. By that time it felt as if there was a thin layer of ice on the outside of my jacket. I once read that the coldest temperature ever recorded on earth was -89.2°C, in Antarctica. I made a mental note to ask Vusi whether he thought zombies could survive in such cold. Maybe they'd freeze, and then Antarctica would be the only safe place to hide from zombies.

I tried to imagine a whole mob of blood-thirsty zombies stalking me and I sawed even faster. Finally, there was a soft click as the saw's blade broke through the shackle.

I opened the padlock and blew on my hands to warm them before pushing the door open with a deafening clank.

The inside of the shed was almost pitch dark, except for two blocks of moonlight falling through the high windows. I closed the door behind me before daring to take the torch from my backpack, and then switched it on. The storeroom looked creepy in the faint light of the torch. Vusi would've been very excited if he could've seen this – at night the shed looked even more perfect for a horror movie. I could easily imagine what it would look like if zombies crawled out of the old Beetle, or from behind the stacked boxes, or maybe one of them could jump from that pile of wooden crates...

Cold shivers ran down my spine when I heard a sudden noise behind me. I swung around just in time to see a large rat scampering away.

Relieved, I exhaled and started searching with the torch. I knew I had better stop thinking

about zombies and simply focus on what I'd come to do. Where would Bruce have hidden the video camera? Maybe close to the music centre?

The first box I opened contained a DVD player and two mobile phones, all still in their original packaging. I couldn't believe that Vusi and Chris and I had been so dumb. We should have realized from the start what was going on. Surely Chris must have known that this wasn't her brother and her uncle's stuff? I wondered when Bruce and his gang were planning to sell these things. And who would buy such a lot of stolen goods?

I rummaged through one box after the other, but found no trace of Vusi's video camera. What if it wasn't even in the shed? Maybe Bruce had decided to keep it for himself.

As I opened a new box, I heard something outside. I froze while staring at the contents of the box.

The rumbling became louder, and then there was the sound of a car engine. A moment later, I heard voices.

With trembling fingers I flicked off the torch.

Car lights appeared under the door. Then the engine was switched off.

In a panic I glanced around in the dark. Where was the best hiding place? Maybe the cupboard? But perhaps they were bringing more stolen stuff to stash in there. Under the Beetle? What if they'd come to steal the car and they drove right over me on their way out?

Then I saw the pile of wooden crates.

Quick as a flash, I grabbed my backpack, dumped the torch inside and zipped it up. I gritted my teeth. With overeager, fumbling fingers, I rummaged through the box before closing it. The crates were stacked to form an almost perfect staircase to the top. The highest crates were nearly right against the roof of the shed. I slung the backpack over my shoulder and started scrambling to the top.

Outside someone was swearing loudly, probably having discovered the broken padlock. The door was pushed open roughly. A torch beam cut through the dark.

'Stay where you are or I'll blow your head off!'

It felt as if my tummy was contracting into a fist. It was Bruce's voice.

'There's no one here, Bruce,' said the dark-haired guy.

To my relief I realized they hadn't seen me. I tried to flatten myself even more on top of the crates.

Below me I could hear Bruce's footsteps on the cement floor.

'Doesn't look like anything's gone,' Bruce said after a while. 'If I get my hands on whoever tried to break in here, he's mincemeat.'

'You think it means someone knows about this place?' The dark-haired man sounded worried. 'We'd better get our merchandise out of here.'

Bruce swore under his breath.

Without warning, I got a very strange feeling. It was as if the earth was starting to give way underneath me. I breathed in sharply and grabbed hold of the edge of a crate to try and keep my balance, but it was too late. The tower of crates tottered, as if in slow motion, and then started tumbling to the ground.

'What the hell?!' I heard Bruce exclaim.

There was a loud bang when I landed on the floor together with a number of crates. A sharp pain shot through my arm. Crates rained down around me for what felt like for ever. When they finally stopped, I cautiously opened my eyes.

A blinding light was shining into my face. It was so bright that I couldn't see Bruce and his gang's faces at all. But I could see the pistol one of them was holding in his hand.

I don't know if it was due to the pain or maybe the shock of having a firearm pointing right into my face, but my head was spinning dangerously. I felt everything around me go dark.

Then a sharp, wailing sound cut through my dizziness. It sounded like...

'Cops!' one of the guys called out in a panic.

Then I understood what was going on: I was dreaming. It was all just a stupid dream. I closed my eyes with a sigh and slept on.

23

Long Numbers That Can Be Divided by Eleven, a Sore Shoulder and Two Policemen

When I opened my eyes, a light was still shining into my face.

'Relax. Don't sit up,' said a voice. 'Tell me, what day of the week is it?'

'Erm...' I swallowed. My throat was bone dry.

'How many fingers do you see?'

'One,' I said in a hoarse voice. I could actually see five fingers, but I assumed the woman meant for me to say how many fingers she was holding up in the air.

'What's four plus seven?'

'Eleven,' I said. 'If you want to find out if a very long number can be divided by eleven, you add up every second digit in the number. Then add up the remaining digits. If the difference between the two answers is zero, or if it's a multiple of eleven...the original number is also…a multiple of eleven.' I coughed. 'May I have some water, please?'

The woman in the white jacket smiled and gave me the glass of water that was standing on the bedside table. She held the straw to my mouth so that I could drink. 'He didn't come off too badly, except for the shoulder. He's still a little confused from the sedative, but he can go home.'

'Thank you, doctor,' said a familiar voice.

I tried to sit up, but it felt as if a giant pair of pliers had my shoulder in a tight grip.

'Take it easy, Clucky. Your shoulder's badly sprained,' Uncle Hendrik said and put his hand on my arm.

I looked down. My arm was in a sling.

'What happened?' I asked, perplexed. Then I remembered the crates starting to fall, the furious voice calling out, the screaming sirens… 'Bruce and those two other guys… Did they…?'

'Hang on,' said Uncle Hendrik patiently. 'The police are waiting outside – they want to ask you some questions. We can talk on the way home. Your mum is frantic with worry.'

When the two policemen walked in, Uncle Hendrik stepped away and sat down on a chair in the corner.

They asked a lot of questions and I told them exactly what had happened. I told them about

Vusi's movie. About Chris, who'd said that she had the perfect place for shooting it. About Bruce and his gang threatening us and taking Vusi's camera. About how I'd decided to go and take it back. The whole time I was speaking, I tried to figure out whether the things I was saying would land Vusi, Chris and me in trouble. But my head felt too fuzzy to think properly.

'You can thank your lucky stars that we arrived in time, laddie!' said the stocky policeman when he finally closed his notebook. 'Things could've turned out very differently.'

'We've been looking for those three guys for a long time,' said his colleague, who had a thin moustache. He turned to Uncle Hendrik. 'He'll have to come into the station later today to make an official statement. But that's all for now.'

After the police had gone, Uncle Hendrik helped me get up off the bed. The hospital was as quiet as a graveyard, except for our footsteps squish-squashing on the grey tiled floor. I looked at my watch. No wonder it was so quiet – it was twenty past four in the morning.

Uncle Hendrik's old pickup was waiting for us in the deserted parking lot. He unlocked the passenger door and put my backpack on the seat before helping me to get in.

'How did the police know they had to go

there?' I asked as we drove out of the hospital gates.

'Long story,' said Uncle Hendrik.

I kept quiet and waited for him to tell me.

'Your mum got up in the night and found this on the kitchen floor...' He took a folded piece of paper from his jacket pocket and gave it to me.

I couldn't believe my eyes when I saw what it was. How on earth did that end up on the kitchen floor? Did it fall out of my backpack? I could have kicked myself.

'Your mum went to your bedroom and saw that you were gone. We looked for you everywhere. Eventually she called Vusi's parents. Vusi spilled the beans about the shed where you guys had been playing in the afternoons, and about Bruce and his mates taking his video camera. Then your mum called the police.'

Uncle Hendrik didn't say another word for the rest of the trip home, as if he wanted to take a break after his long explanation.

When we approached our house, I saw that all the lights were on. I sighed. Obviously I was in major trouble.

'What else is in your backpack?' Uncle Hendrik asked when we stopped next to the house.

I smiled as I remembered. That was the one good thing that had happened tonight...

24

Puffy Eyes and a Conversation on a Veranda

That Monday and Tuesday I didn't go to school.

Mum refused to let me set foot outside the house, except on Sunday afternoon when Uncle Hendrik took me to the police station to make a statement.

Cindy also stayed at home. She locked herself inside her room, and when she finally joined us for breakfast on Tuesday morning after Mum threatened to break down her door, her eyes were still puffy from crying.

Uncle Hendrik said that Bruce and his gang didn't get bail – the police had told him that. They wanted to arrest the rest of the syndicate before they'd consider releasing Bruce on bail.

I didn't know what to say to Cindy. It didn't sound right to say that I was sorry. After all, her boyfriend had threatened to kill me – not once but *twice*.

It was only late that Tuesday afternoon that I got a chance to sneak out of the house. My backpack kept banging against my back while I rode to Vusi's house. It was a bit tricky keeping my bike on the road with my arm still in the sling.

When I rang the doorbell, it almost felt like the first time. After Cheetah had bitten and killed Kathleen.

Vusi's mum opened the door. 'Clucky,' she said.

I swallowed nervously. From the way she said my name, I immediately knew she had a lot of things to say to me. Not very friendly things. Things like: '*Why did you make a movie on the sly with my son, even though you knew he was sick?*' Or: '*Get lost, and never set foot here again!*'

But I beat her to it.

'Ma'am, I just want to say that I'm very, very sorry about what happened.'

When she opened her mouth to say something, I beat her to it again.

'But, actually, I'm not really sorry. Vusi desperately wanted to make a movie. And I just wanted to help him. Chris *and* I. And nothing that happened was Chris's fault because she actually didn't know that Vusi was sick. And...'

Suddenly I dried up. I unzipped my backpack. 'And I just wanted to return Vusi's video camera.'

I hadn't told the police that I'd found the camera. Just before I scrambled up the crates to flee from Bruce and his gang, I saw it inside the last box and quickly grabbed it. I wasn't sure whether removing something from a crime scene was completely legal, but I guessed it couldn't be *completely* illegal – after all, it was Vusi's camera.

'And I also brought this,' I said and thrust a piece of paper into her hand. It was the last flyer. I'd distributed all the others.

When I'd said everything that I wanted to say, I turned around and walked to my bike, which was leaning against the gatepost. Riding off, I didn't dare look around to see what Vusi's mum was doing.

I wished I had the courage to ride to Chris's house as well.

When I got home, the newspaper was lying on the table. On the front page was a headline that said: *Gang of robbers caught thanks to schoolchildren.*

25

Zombies

Before I knew it, it was Saturday afternoon. The moment I had been waiting for all week.

When I arrived at the park, there was only one person there. Feeling disappointed, I got off my bike, taking care not to hurt my shoulder. Sitting on the small bench next to the rubbish bin was a slender figure wearing a floral dress and a Frankenstein mask.

'Clucky,' she said when I approached her.

'Aunt Hantie?' I asked, gobsmacked.

'How do I look?' she asked and turned her head so that I could admire the mask. 'I found it among the children's old toys. It's hard to throw those things away, you know. Sentimental value.'

'Erm...actually it's supposed to be a zombie, Auntie.'

She took the mask off, looking taken aback. 'So what is this thing then?'

'It's Frankenstein's monster, Auntie. But never mind – we can put make-up on you.'

She put the mask down next to her and dug something out of her handbag. Screwing up her eyes, she unfolded a sheet of paper and studied it. I peeped over her shoulder, even though I knew the contents by heart.

WANNA BE IN A MOVIE?

This is your chance!

We're making a horror movie and we need ZOMBIES!

Where: the park opposite the library

When: Saturday 24 July

Time: 17:00

(Bring your own zombie mask if you have one!)

Clucky, Vusi & Chris

Nearly a week had passed since I rode around on my bike in the freezing dead of night, putting the flyers into people's letter boxes. Maybe everyone had forgotten about it.

Aunt Hantie unwrapped a piece of chewing gum. 'I saw in the paper that the three of you are heroes now. I can't believe you finally nabbed that Bruce and his mates. I've known for a long time that that scoundrel was up to no good. He and that Lategan boy who landed up in jail – you know, Chris's brother – were always loitering around, looking for trouble. I heard rumours that the Lategan boy was also involved in all this, even though he's in jail.'

I shook my head. 'That isn't true, Auntie. The police said Chris's brother was innocent. He didn't know that Bruce and his cronies were using the shed to store their stolen goods.'

Aunt Hantie stared at me in silence while slowly chewing her gum. That hardly ever happened: Aunt Hantie not saying anything. 'You like that girl, don't you, Clucky?' she said after a while.

My face was hot. 'She...she's very angry at Vusi and me.' I changed the subject. 'I don't think she's ever going to speak to me again.'

The past three days at school and on the bus, Chris hadn't even looked my way, never mind spoken to me. She was terribly good at ignoring people when she was mad. I hadn't heard from Vusi either after visiting their house on Tuesday.

Aunt Hantie smiled. 'She's a feisty one. But don't give up hope.' She spat out the piece of gum and threw it in the rubbish bin. 'You must remember, Clucky, people react differently when they're hurt. Some get cocky and hope that will protect them against more hurt. Others go into hiding because they're too scared of getting hurt again.' She took a fresh piece of gum from her pocket but didn't unwrap it.

'You're a good boy, Clucky. That's the only reason why I decided to come when I found the flyer in my letter box. I don't even like those spooky horror movies.'

I looked again at the paper in her hand. 'I don't think anyone else is going to show up,' I said in dismay. 'And I don't even think Vusi's mum will allow *him* to come.'

'I'm not so sure about that,' said Aunt Hantie.

I gave her a puzzled look. Then I saw what she was looking at. A car was approaching. Vusi's dad's Mercedes. His dad got out first, then Vusi and then his mum and Miranda. Vusi had his backpack and his camera with him.

Aunt Hantie and I watched in silence as they crossed the lawn towards us.

'Three zombies reporting for duty,' Vusi's dad said to me and put his arm around his wife's waist.

Miranda smiled that smile of hers that made you feel slightly shaky.

'We'll have to change the entire story,' Vusi said. He smiled at me. 'But that's OK.'

Just then there was a loud bang from the direction of the street.

Surprised, I asked Vusi, 'Is that the school bus?'

He shrugged.

The rattletrap bus drove right up to us and stopped in a cloud of smoke. One by one, the plot plodders got out: Patrick with his thick glasses, Safraaz, Waylon, even the blonde twins, Mandi and Jolandi. I swallowed hard when Chris also appeared from the bus. Last but not least, Mr Oldman got out.

'Do you have a role for a one-armed zombie?' he asked.

Vusi looked at me and a big smile lit up his face. 'Of course, sir,' he said. 'You're perfect!'

Safraaz grunted. 'I only came along because my dad told me to. Because you guys helped catch those guys who broke into our cafe twice.'

'Thanks,' I said.

Safraaz sighed. 'My dad said he'd bring us all some cold drinks and snacks later on. I just have to call him on my mobile and let him know how many people we are.'

Two more cars approached and stopped next to the school bus.

'I hope your dad knows what he's let himself in for,' Aunt Hantie said drily to Safraaz. 'Seems like we're going to have a whole horde of zombies!'

I looked at Chris. She was standing a little way off, with her back to us. I summoned up all my courage and went over to her.

'I'm so sorry about everything.'

She turned around. 'Actually, *I* have to say sorry. I shouldn't have gone off like that. It was just...'

'That's OK,' I said. 'C'mon, we have to start making up the zombies before it gets too dark.'

Vusi was already explaining to people what they should do. When Chris and I approached, he started giving us orders as well.

More people joined us. At five sharp, I counted thirty-one people.

With a gesture, Vusi gathered everyone around him. When they all grew quiet, he started to explain the story behind the movie.

'We're going to shoot the last scene of the movie first. With a mob of zombies sweeping down on Chris and me. Then we're going to open fire... We'll decide which of you will be shot dead.'

'But then how are we going to gobble you up?' asked Mr Oldman. He let out a spine-chilling zombie roar.

Everyone laughed.

Vusi shook his head. 'No, Chris and I will escape. But one of the zombies is going to bite me. Clucky, that'll be you. And then I have to say goodbye to Chris at the end of the movie before I also turn into a zombie.'

Aunt Hantie shuddered. 'It sounds like a terribly bloody affair. Are you sure there–'

She stopped speaking suddenly. It looked as if her mouth had fallen open with amazement.

Chris softly put her hand on my shoulder. 'Clucky, look...'

I turned around slowly.

The last time my mum had left the house was two years, four months and nineteen days ago. That was how long ago my dad was buried.

Everyone watched in silence as Mum walked towards us over the lawn. On her left walked Uncle Hendrik and on her right was Cindy. It looked like Mum could feel every inquisitive eye on her but she resolutely kept walking towards us.

Cindy's eyes were still a little puffy, but she was smiling. I almost couldn't remember when I last saw my sister smile. 'I came to help,' she said. 'Last term we did special effects make-up at the college. Zombie make-up can't be that difficult.'

'And I haven't been in a movie for years,' Mum said, 'but I'll try my best. That is, if you have a part for an old has-been like me...'

Then she smiled and pulled me close to her. And only then did I realize she was wearing Dad's leather jacket.

26

Einstein, Time and Another Newspaper Article

Einstein said that time is relative. I knew this wasn't what he meant, but when lots of things are happening and you're busy all the time, you sometimes don't even notice how quickly time passes.

Winter passed, and then spring, and then it was summer. The year had nearly come to an end. Soon we would start taking our exams, and after that the long-awaited December holidays would follow.

Late one afternoon I popped in to visit Vusi. A pigeon was cooing high up in a tree and somewhere in the distance you could hear children playing and laughing.

As usual, I sat down next to him.

'I went for another advanced maths lesson this afternoon,' I said. 'It was really tough, but a thousand times more fun than Mr Faure's maths classes.'

I hardly believed my ears the day the headmaster summoned me to tell me about the extra maths lessons. Miss Cullen, the student teacher who was doing her practical at our school, had found the page on which I did sums that afternoon in detention. I hadn't known that the sums were part of an old university paper. She showed the page to one of her lecturers at university, and they then invited me to become part of a programme for people who liked maths a lot. We met every Friday afternoon. Miss Cullen came to pick me up in her car. I was one of only two schoolchildren – the rest of the class consisted of university students.

'I have big news...' I said to Vusi. 'Miranda came to visit Uncle Hendrik. And I saw him kissing her when she left!'

The evening we shot the final scene of the zombie movie, Uncle Hendrik and Miranda had started chatting to each other. At first I thought my eyes were deceiving me because Uncle Hendrik had always been so shy, but maybe all the laughing and chatting zombies around him had made him come out of his shell. Or maybe it had just been Miranda. She was still one of the most beautiful women I'd ever seen. I still struggled to speak when she was around.

I started telling Vusi about the things that had happened at school.

'Chris and I are working on an Afrikaans project together. We have to do something on an author.' I laughed. 'We're still fighting about who we're going to choose.'

A few weeks before his death, Vusi finally admitted that Miranda had told him that Mum used to be an actress. Miranda in turn had heard it from Mrs Moosa from the cafe. And everyone knew that there was nothing that Mrs Moosa didn't know about other people's affairs.

'Oh yes, I have more great news,' I said. 'My mum got a job at a radio station. She says they won't pay her much, but she's going to host a chat programme every weekday.'

In the beginning it had been strange to come and chat to Vusi like this. But after the second or third time I'd grown used to it.

I was in school the morning he died. His mum and dad and Miranda were with him. The doctors hadn't thought that it would happen that quickly, but one day he suddenly took a turn for the worse. He had to be taken to hospital, where he stayed for the last three weeks of his life.

Before he died, I convinced his mum and dad to rent a movie projector and one evening we invited everyone in the cancer ward to come and watch *The End of the World*. Even the doctors and nurses joined us – and, of course, Chris and Mum and Uncle Hendrik and Cindy and Miranda and Aunt Hantie. Everyone laughed a lot and Aunt Hantie shut her eyes tightly every time a zombie appeared on the screen. (But she *did* peep when she was hobbling across the screen herself – with a hideous, blood-smeared face, thanks to Cindy's scary make-up.) At the end of the movie, everyone clapped and cheered and congratulated Vusi. I could see that he was very, very proud.

A light breeze was blowing through the trees. I looked at my watch.

When I got up, I felt in my trouser pocket to make sure the newspaper clipping was still there.

'I have to go now,' I told Vusi's gravestone. 'There's something else I still have to do.'

Ever since that evening when I lay on my bed thinking about it, I thought of death as zero. Zero isn't the end – it's the middle. It's halfway between the positive and the negative numbers – on either side of zero are two rows of numbers that extend to infinity, far enough to make you dizzy with excitement.

I never told anyone about that. It was just my way of seeing it. Maybe Mum and Cindy and Uncle Hendrik all thought of it in different ways.

Just as there are different ways to do a difficult sum.

I slowly walked through the rows of gravestones. Past forty gravestones, then left and past another eleven.

I stopped in front of a simple black marble slab. For a while I just stared at the name and the dates that were engraved into the marble with white letters.

'I finally saved up enough egg money, Dad,' I said. 'To buy computers for the school. But don't worry – I'm still selling eggs. Aunt Hantie said Safraaz's dad's cafe has become even more expensive.'

I unfolded the newspaper clipping, bent down and put it under the vase with the plastic flowers. I looked at it for a moment, then turned around and walked back to where my bike was leaning against the tree, waiting.

SCHOOL PUZZLED OVER ANONYMOUS DONATION

The headmaster and governing body of Rocklands Primary are elated about a mysterious donation their school received this week. Out of the blue, a consignment of ten new computers was delivered to the school, but the name of the donor is unknown. The company the computers were bought from said the donor has asked to remain anonymous.

'It's still a complete mystery,' the delighted headmaster, Mr Devon Claasen, said yesterday morning. 'But we are very grateful for this donation because our students badly need exposure to the latest computer technology.'

Apparently the government had provided funds for a computer centre two years ago, but on its way to the school the original consignment of computers was destroyed in a collision.

Acknowledgements

While, sadly, I did not inherit my dad's amazing maths skills (ask my high-school maths teachers), there are countless other ways in which he has inspired me – and we're both very fond of chickens. Thanks for always believing in me, Dad, and for allowing me to pursue my dreams.

Elize, Mia and Emma, thank you for being patient those days when I'm counting chickens in my head. I love you gazillions.

This book would not have been possible without the hard work and encouragement of Miemie du Plessis, my publisher, friend – and also a maths whizz, who helped check Clucky's sums in this book.

A big shout-out to Lizé Vosloo, Stefan Enslin, Morné du Toit and the rest of the team responsible for the film adaptation of this book, released in South Africa in 2017.

Thank you to Kobus Geldenhuys for the wonderful English translation and to Madeleine Stevens for the sharp-eyed copy-editing – it's an absolute pleasure working with both of you.

And last but certainly not least, thank you to my editor, Shadi Doostdar, as well as Paul Nash, Kate Bland, Harriet Wade and the rest of the team at Oneworld and Rock the Boat. If I ever had to face a zombie horde, I would be lucky to have a crew like you by my side.

Also by Jaco Jacobs,

A GOOD DAY FOR CLIMBING TREES

Translated by Kobus Geldenhuys

Illustrations by Jim Tierney

'Quirky, charming and very funny, but with a real emotional
punch. It is the perfect place to start for someone looking
to move on from *The Wimpy Kid* books.'
Anthony McGowan, author of *The Donut Diaries*

HOW TWO UNLIKELY HEROES INSPIRE
A TOWN BY FIGHTING TO SAVE A TREE

Sometimes, in the blink of an eye, you do something that
changes your life forever.

Like climbing a tree with a girl you don't know.

Marnus is tired of feeling invisible, living in the
shadow of his two brothers.

His older brother is good at breaking swimming records and girls' hearts.
His younger brother is already a crafty entrepreneur who has tricked
him into doing the dishes all summer. But when a girl called Leila turns
up on their doorstep one morning with a petition, it's the start of an
unexpected adventure.

Finally, Marnus gets the chance to be noticed...

Stay up to date with all news from the boat @rocktheboatnews